Journal of
Eva Morelli

Journal of Eva Morelli

Maryann D'Agincourt

PP

Portmay Press
New York

Cover design by Patricia Fabricant.

Cover image credit: *Undergrowth with Two Figures*, 1890 (oil on canvas), Gogh, Vincent van (1853-90) / Cincinnati Art Museum, Ohio, USA / Bequest of Mary E. Johnston / The Bridgeman Art Library.

Excerpt from *The Bay of Noon* by Shirley Hazzard. Copyright © 1970 by Shirley Hazzard. Reprinted by permission of Picador and the author.

The line from *Ghosts* is taken from *Four Major Plays, Volume II* by Henrik Ibsen, translated by Rolf Fjelde, published by Signet Classics.

Printed in the United States of America

First printing, 2013

Publisher's Cataloging-in-Publication
(Provided by Quality Books, Inc.)

D'Agincourt, Maryann.
        Journal of Eva Morelli / Maryann D'Agincourt.
        p. cm.
        ISBN 978-0-9891745-0-3
        ISBN 978-0-9891745-1-0 (ebook)

        1. Psychiatrists--Fiction. 2. Physician and patient --Fiction. 3. Psychological fiction. 4. Domestic fiction. 5. Diary fiction. I. Title..
PS3604.A3325J68 2013   813'.6
                                  QBI13-600066

PP Portmay Press
     244 Madison Avenue
     New York, NY 10016
     www.portmaypress.com

For Paul

With sincere thanks to Sandra Birdsell, Rosemary James, Emily Albarillo, and Antanas Sileika.

"One can only discover what has already come into existence."
—Shirley Hazzard, *The Bay of Noon*

One

Eva, early June

Her full name is Eva Morelli Stein Hathaway. She retains all her surnames not because they define her, but because she defines them; that is, except the first—Morelli. Ironically it is the one she's least familiar with.

Sorrow has transformed her features, refining her cheekbones, softening her more blue than gray eyes. Yet boldness is revealed in her arched brows, vulnerability in her narrow chin.

On this warm June morning, a soft wind billows her scarf as she mounts the front steps of a four-story brick building. Firmly she turns the knob of the heavy oak door and pushes it open. She glances at the spacious lobby, the high ceiling, the hardwood flooring. Her heart begins to race, as if she's about to approach the witness stand, all eyes upon her. But soon she's facing a wide ascending stairway with red carpeting, and she is alone.

As she grasps the banister, she sees how her hand slightly trembles, yet she takes the first step.

Halfway up she grows doubtful; she doesn't know if this is an exercise in deceit or a quest for truth. Momentarily she thinks of Bill, the curve of his upper lip, his solidity, and how until recently she believed their marriage was her solution. She pauses, asks herself: Am I courageous? Destructive? How will it end?

What is most important is not one of those questions, she realizes, but her compelling desire to go through with it. Quickly she climbs up the remaining steps.

When she reaches the top of the stairway, she looks across the hall; her eyes fasten on the gold plaque nailed to the door.

Etched in black lettering:

Stephen Forester, M.D.
    Psychiatry

Softly Eva speaks, reading the sign, her mouth numbing. His name is like a magnet; she goes to the door, opens it, and stands on the threshold, her eyes searching. No one else is in the waiting room. The sound of trickling water unnerves her; she sees a small fish tank tucked in a corner on top of a low table, and chooses the seat farthest away from it.

As apprehensive as she is, the calm of the waiting room affects her and she begins to relax. It simply looks like the outer room of any physician's office, yet she supposes much time and thought have gone into decorating it. The purpose of its design—is it to create a haven for patients before they enter what she imagines will be a somber main office with dark leather furniture to reveal their fears and desires?

More composed, she studies Stephen Forester's diplomas from medical school and residency on the wall; her eyes narrow as she tries to decipher the lettering, a dark curving scroll. Then she turns her attention to the bookcase, the softcover orange medical journals, the heavy, hardbound psychiatric texts, and spread across the lower two shelves, contemporary magazines, the *New Yorker*, *Architectural Digest*, and *Better Homes and Gardens*.

The only picture in the room is a copy of *Undergrowth with Two Figures* by Van Gogh. The painting reminds Eva of her parents, how they were when she was a child. The man and woman are walking through what she intuitively calls "the woods," their arms linked. The moss-green color of the woman's dress is the same green as the Oriental rug on the floor of the waiting room, and both the painting and rug have flecks of yellow-gold. The man and woman are tall and slender, though her mother was small and firm. The woman is reminiscent of her mother in that she appears the sturdier of the two, yet only slightly so, while the man is thin and tall like her father was, his shoulders narrow and square; it's as if he's about to be blown over by a strong wind.

Her eyes mist. Seeking justice will uncover the truth, she affirms, as she hears the main office door click open.

Two

Brea, early June

"How is your husband the shrink?" Sam asks.

Brea sits on a high stool opposite him on the dark oval-shaped stage, her legs tightly crossed as she looks up at the lone light on in the dark theater. Sarcasm, she thinks, attracted to his tone, pleased no one else is there.

"Nice of you to ask, Sam—he's fine. But we haven't come here to talk about Stephen," she says in a low voice.

"Yes, Brea—the summer production."

She's worked with him ever since she moved with her husband and son to this small New Hampshire town on the coast, one hour from Boston. Sam is different from the directors in New York, much more matter-of-fact in his approach, in his interpretation of a play. She accepts it, as she's been able to take on more interesting roles. But she's growing weary of Harrington, and Sam's literal technique.

As he gets off his stool and begins to pace, her gaze lingers on his tall, sturdy form, his slightly bent head, his straight hair nearly touching his shoulders. He stops, turns to look at her. "I've decided against Chekhov—I'd rather do Ibsen. What do you think?" he asks, his expression pleading.

To Brea his eyes are like swirling brown shells, inscrutable and hard. He comes to her, presses her shoulders with firm hands, urgently, insistently, as he's done many times before. Yet for the first time she feels uneasy, thinking of how in the past she's observed other actresses fall for him.

As he continues to pace, she says hastily, "Ibsen is fine, but I do prefer Chekhov's *Three Sisters*—it's provocative, definite."

"That's your Russian heritage speaking," he answers, looking over at her.

"Half Russian," she says directly, meeting his gaze. She turns away, ruffles her short, dark hair. "But on second thought I do like Ibsen too—haven't done one of his plays in so long—yes—Ibsen."

She looks down at her watch. Ned will be out early from school, and the two of them plan to meet Stephen at his office for lunch.

"You need to pick up Ned?" Sam asks.

She nods.

"Go on, then."

"You know I need time to prepare for the role, Sam," she says, sliding off the stool.

"But of course, Brea."

Her name sounds strange coming from him. He says it too curtly, she thinks. Yet early in life she learned her name was open to interpretation. It suggested different things to different people. Brea isn't a neutral-sounding name, like Tom, Mary, or Jane; people are never diverted by such names.

She gives a person whatever their interpretation of a Brea is, as a mirror does a reflection; she understands what is perceived isn't who she really is, but an imagined "Brea." To some, the name suggests an impulsive nature; to those like her mother, it suggests authority; and to certain past lovers, it implied passion.

Brea knows she assumes these roles, but she can't help herself. It's as if she is protecting the other person; from what, she isn't certain. She supposes they see reflections of themselves in her gaze.

Quickly she kisses Sam good-bye, and then makes her way down the dark aisle, feeling the impression of the corner of his mouth on her lips. When she opens the theater door, she's nearly blinded by the sun. The temperature has risen abruptly in the last hour—too warm for early June, she thinks.

As she drives through town on her way to pick up Ned from school, she eyes the small shops on Main Street, the white gazebo in the center of the square. It no longer appears as quaint as it once did, but dull, too pristine, small, uninspiring.

Not Chekhov, but Ibsen, she thinks, and makes associations beginning with Chekhov and leading to that late September day ten years ago when she and Stephen left New York City in their hunter-green Volvo, loaded with odds and ends the moving company had not taken. Two-year-old Ned in his car seat wailed as he'd never done before. Brea felt raw, filled with misgivings as she looked out at the usually dull waters of the East River now sparkling in the early autumn light.

They were leaving the only life she'd known. She took a deep breath; the life she'd led in New York would no longer be available to her.

She'd spent years in the theater in New York, an understudy mostly, yet from time to time she'd had the opportunity to act in off-Broadway productions of Chekhov, Wilde and Shakespeare. No longer! They were moving to a small, quaint town in New Hampshire where Stephen would have his own practice. No longer would he spend countless hours working in a locked unit of a psychiatric hospital, disgruntled about ordering physical restraints on patients. In their new life, she'd act in a small theater near the rugged coast, with opportunities for more varied roles, and Stephen would have more time for his writing.

Suddenly the East River was no longer in view, and it struck her that this new life they'd imagined for a year now, a quiet, more subdued existence where they'd be able to throw themselves into their work, could turn out to be an illusion. Why did this occur to her only now? Had they acted without thinking? They'd always been cautious in their decisions.

"Stephen," she asked in a low, steady voice, "are we making a mistake?'

"Change is good. We'll broaden ourselves. And if we don't like our new life, we can always come back to New York. We have more control over this decision than you realize," he said, running his fingers down the side of his face, his other hand loosely guiding the steering wheel.

And as always she was buoyed by his words—that was why she'd agreed to marry him. He believed in her and her ability to direct her own life.

They were past their twenties when they met, having found one another a little later—it was because of their demanding careers and immersion in city life. Yet when Ned was born, they wanted him to have light and space, a sense of physical freedom, something he couldn't have if he grew up in the city, something neither she nor Stephen had experienced. She had been born and raised in New York, Stephen in Boston. And when the towers so brutally had came down a year after they left New York, she was convinced it had been the right decision—they'd escaped, and that sense of rightness had lasted until now.

After living ten years in Harrington, where restaurants do not remain open through the early morning hours, where people stay ensconced in their homes most evenings, what have they gained? How quickly the time has passed! Ned is neither a country boy nor a city boy, he is stuck somewhere in the middle. When Stephen and she are away, he prefers to be with his grandmother in New York. And when the three of them go to the city during a long holiday weekend he's always very content. Ned doesn't truly fit in either place and he's growing more and more wistful because of it, she believes.

Because Stephen's work is tiring, his writing is moving at a snail's pace. Yes, every summer he presents a paper on his latest thoughts and findings in one European city or another, but it's progressing very slowly.

Abruptly Brea turns the steering wheel to the right, driving away from the town center. And she asks herself: What do I have?

Yes, she's been able to act in varied and exciting roles. But how appreciative is her Harrington audience? It isn't that they aren't well read, or interested in Chekhov, Ibsen, or Shakespeare; it's simply that they aren't New Yorkers, for whom, she earnestly believes, theater genuinely matters.

Such thoughts have occurred to her before, but never with the same urgency. It's because she was drawn to Sam today, she ruefully thinks, feeling the same angst she experienced when she left New York ten years ago. And suddenly she realizes how much she longs for the city where she was born, grew up and lived most of her adult life, her city, as once before she yearned for a lover. They must go back, she thinks, her heart pounding. She'll tell Stephen immediately.

An image of Sam crosses her mind. He's standing before her, his arms extended, his expression beguiling. Insidious, she thinks, and feels a sudden weakness, a yearning for what she knows she doesn't want. As she shakes this picture from her mind, she decides that when they reach Stephen's office she will have Ned sit in the waiting room while she talks with Stephen about her desire to return to New York. Because she isn't impulsive, he'll take her request seriously. She believes that even with his accepting nature, he doesn't truly feel settled here. He's discontented; she sees this from the restless way he goes through the travel section of the newspaper, how he hasn't bothered to garden, something he'd planned to do when they first moved to Harrington, and how he has kept up his professional contacts in New York and Boston, never really establishing any in the vicinity of Harrington.

He'll understand, she thinks. She's suppressed these feelings for so long. And because he's more methodical than she is, he'll know what steps to take. They'll work together and turn their life back to what it was.

When she stops the car in front of the school, she sees Ned a few feet away, talking to a friend, his blond hair catching the light. She gets out of the car. Warmly she calls out to him.

Three

Stephen, early June

The blinds in Stephen's office are half-drawn, the windows opened, a breeze rustles the papers on his desk. He sits in a low chair alongside his desk, leaning slightly forward, listening attentively to Eva Hathaway, a new patient. She sits opposite him, and he's aware she's swaying slightly in the swivel chair.

Her hands clasped on her lap, she's dressed in a black-and-white cotton skirt, a black top, and a silk scarf closely replicating the design in her skirt, which reminds him of the swirling pattern on the front side of a deck of cards. On the fourth finger of her left hand is a rectangular emerald, no diamonds, no other jewelry. He finds her bearing distinguished, as if she's traveled much, having viewed the world and its complexities at close range. However, she lives in this small New Hampshire town. Stephen is accustomed to seeing people with exotic backgrounds settling in Harrington, but he's learned over the ten years of his practice here that most have a past of some sort, something they are running from.

When he asks her date of birth, she says the eleventh of September, neglecting to give the year, lightly touching the knot in her scarf and meeting his gaze.

"I'm having a dream, a recurring one," she'd told him in a wistful voice when she called to set up the appointment a few weeks before. "I need help with it." Then she sighed and said, "It's affecting my life." For a brief moment she sounded as if she might weep. They set up a date for her to come in to see him.

When Stephen ended the call, he couldn't help but smile. No one wanted to talk about dreams anymore; most patients came to him for some new medication they'd read about online that eases anxiety or depression. He appreciated her earnestness in the face of her unease, but he did not make any assumptions about this new patient or read into what she said. His strength as a psychiatrist is to avoid drawing easy conclusions.

He forgot about her phone call in the intervening weeks. This morning when he saw her name on the appointment list, he didn't remember her story.

Now he turns to the side and pulls out the intake sheet from the folder on his desk. As he reviews it, he recalls their phone conversation. After he finishes reading, he looks up, notices her deep-set eyes are an unsteady blue, and fleetingly he thinks of the Adriatic, the summer when he was ten and went to Bari for two weeks with his father, never questioning the absence of his eager and shyly doting mother.

Mrs. Hathaway raises her narrow chin and says, "I've been having this dream for about six months now. Though it is the same dream, each time there are different people in it, some I know and others I don't recognize. The first time, my husband and I were in it. We danced on a black-and-white tiled floor in evening dress. The ballroom was large, five chandeliers, glittering light. He wore a tuxedo and I was in a pale blue gown. There were many people about, but we were the only ones dancing. I couldn't hear any music, but we continued to dance. No one acknowledged us—it was as if we were not there."

Her eyes are now tear-filled, luminous, and he understands it is difficult for her to continue. Humbly he waits out her silence as he was taught by his father, Dr. Arthur Forester, a renowned Boston analyst in his time. He'd told Stephen that it is a privilege, an honor really, to hear someone's revelations. "Stephen, you must respect, but be aware of what is omitted; therein lies the truth," his father had instructed him in his painstaking way. Though his father has been dead for many years, his words weave in and out of Stephen's mind like prayers that no longer have meaning, only resonance. If his father hadn't said those words, he'd still be respectful; deference comes as naturally to Stephen as his mellow regard for the subjects in Van Gogh's paintings.

Stephen shifts his lanky frame, crosses his legs, and she continues slowly, less confidently, he thinks. "I felt the floor tilting, and when I looked round everyone had vanished except Bill, and we continued to dance. Yet he wasn't aware of the tilting floor. When I tried to tell him, I couldn't speak; it was as if I were suffocating—and then water began pouring onto the dance floor. This is when I wake up in a cold sweat. You see, I've developed a fear of water; I was unable to go in the ocean last February when we were in Miami. I'm uneasy taking a shower; I need to leave the door open. Yet, as I said, it isn't always my husband in the dream; it can be friends, or people I haven't seen in the longest time. If I am not dancing in the dream, I am observing the couple. I watch coldly as the floor starts to tilt."

Visibly shaken, she clenches her fists. Her eyes are still moist, her lashes wet, her pupils receding into the blue. She raises herself a bit off the seat to adjust her skirt.

When she seems composed, he asks, "How often does it occur?"

"Once, maybe twice a week."

"When did you become fearful of water—how long after you began to have this dream?"

"Slowly . . . I wasn't conscious of having this fear immediately. I became aware of it the day I realized I needed to leave the door open when taking a shower. It was about a month after I first had the dream. Bill, who was trying to listen to the news on the TV in the bedroom, shut the door. I panicked and got out of the shower, nearly slipping on the floor."

He nods and jots down some notes on the intake sheet. "What does it mean to you?" he asks.

"The dream?" she says.

"I mean, having this fear," he answers.

"I've always thought of myself as a brave person—
it's surprising to have a fear—a silly one at that. I've
never really been afraid of anything before. It's as if
what I've always believed about myself isn't true." She
appears pensive. And he senses complex levels of
thought in her tone.

"You may want to keep a journal close to your bed
so that when you wake you can record the details of
your dream."

He also suggests a medication to help with her
anxiety.

"I do not want a bandage," she says forcefully, re-
fusing him, and he sees that she's regained her confidence. "I want to know the truth," she says.

"The truth," he repeats, hearing detachment in his
voice. He closes his lips and meets her gaze. Her brows
are slightly raised, as if in some way he's disappointed
her, he thinks.

Her session has come to an end, so they establish a
date for another appointment. He opens the door of his
office for her, and when, moments later, he hears her
walking down the stairs, he is uneasy.

For the past few weeks he's had a pressing sense
that something is missing. It isn't an object he's mis-
placed, or a person he has lost; in his careful and penetrating way he's convinced it is because his life is
somehow incomplete. This belief took root on a rainy
mid-May evening as he got into his car to drive home
from work. Beyond the wet glistening street and across
the misty square, there was a boy of about eight or
nine, banging on the door of a women's clothing store
that was apparently closed. There was no one else in
sight. After fiddling to fasten his seat belt, he looked

up; the child was gone. And he became unnerved. These past two weeks he's been unable to shed this sensation; it has awakened within him an angst that in his adult life has been foreign to him.

As he begins to type notes on his laptop, it strikes him that Eva Hathaway reminds him of someone—her appearance, not necessarily her manner or demeanor.

He stops typing, takes off his glasses, and rapidly taps his fist on the desk again and again. Then it comes to him. Vaguely she resembles the babysitter who cared for him for a few years when he was a child; she taught him about humor, about hope, his parents having been such serious people. So long ago. He wonders what happened to her. Her name—Italian—he cannot recall. If she's alive, she must be nearly ninety.

A car door opens and shuts. He gets up from his chair and pulls up the blinds. Brea and Ned, his wife and son, walk across the parking lot toward his office building. He presses one hand to the warm pane. What he's been remembering slips away. A light, caressing breeze touches his cheek; he cannot help but smile.

Eva's Journal

Dr. Forester was different than I thought he'd be, soft-spoken, subtle, his pale green eyes gentle but at times so intense, his hair a reddish-blond color, too fine and short to be parted. The expression on his narrow face was solemn, his lips mostly closed, pensively so, as if he were making an effort to slow or monitor his emotions.

I neither liked nor distained him. And though I told the truth, I was essentially fiction. Did he know the difference? It went better than I expected. But now that I've left him, I realize I am as lost as if I have landed in an unknown country without my phone or luggage.

I must sustain myself, hold myself up, recover, and most importantly, recreate myself. I'll not write about my dreams as he suggested. I'll write to reconstruct what I've destroyed. I'll go to what I remember, start at the beginning, see who I was, get to who I am, what I've become.

Four

Brea, her brown eyes still, sits in Stephen's office leaning back expectantly, dressed in the cornflower blue top and Capri pants he bought for her last summer in Stockholm. But he notices how tightly her hands grip the arms of the swivel chair.

"Stephen, it struck me today how suffocating it is in Harrington," she says.

"Suffocating," he repeats, dismayed by her words, shutting down the laptop on his desk.

He gets up, goes over to the window, and closes the blinds. When he turns back he sees her lips trembling slightly. "Who is suffocating you, Brea?"

"No one. It's life, here. There is really nothing for me to do!"

He remembers her enthusiasm when they first moved to Harrington; she loved their new home, spacious, unlike anything you'd find in the city, she'd said. And the theater, so close to the ocean, only a fifteen-minute walk from where they lived—she'd been elated. He pictures her standing outside the playhouse that first day, staring out at the water, her arms crossed, a breeze blowing her cropped hair, her eyes gleaming.

"But your work—you have that. And Ned," he says, purposely not mentioning himself. For between them he believes he's the one who loves more.

"Of course," she says. "But I think we should seriously consider returning to New York. After meeting with Sam today, I had—I guess you would call it—a moment of clarity. I miss city life. And I am tired of performing in his plays. I still want to act, but not here."

She stands up and continues, "Aside from my need to go back to New York, I believe there is something wrong with the three of us living in Harrington—but can't put my finger on exactly what it is."

He goes over to her and stands close, holding her gaze. "What is it, Brea? What's bothering you?"

"You look puzzled, Stephen. Are you happy in Harrington?" she asks pointedly.

"You and Ned are here," he answers.

"Oh, Stephen," she says piquantly, stroking one side of his face; he's warmed by her touch yet catches a whiff of something unfamiliar—a sharp, pungent scent, not her cologne. Sam's? he wonders, his heart beating quickly.

She turns away, and he takes a deep breath. He hears a knock on the door.

"It's Ned. Let's go," she says hastily.

He nods. Brea is edgy. He hasn't seen this side of her in so long, he thinks, switching off the lights as he follows her out of the office.

Eva's Journal

I remember the day in images, rich but fleeting—my heart pounded as my mother carried me in her arms. I wore a red flannel dress, matching ankle socks and a woolen jacket. A November day, the air was cold against my face and bare legs, my chest warm from Mother's embrace. Carrying me in her arms, she rushed to the store where my father worked. Her expression was frightened, her eyes like dark knobs. I remember her being small and willful. That day, her complexion was ruddy from the cold, tiny faint freckles were sprinkled across her nose and cheeks. I felt frantic motion in her hurried steps and feared I'd fall out of her arms. I let out a cry. "Hush, Eva, hush," she said in her stern, raspy voice, her breath hot against my neck. She grasped an envelope tightly in one hand. I glimpsed large slanted handwriting in blue ink. Over her shoulder I saw people waving, calling out, "Rose, Rose, are you okay?"

She ignored them and held me close, her chin resting sharply on my shoulder, pinning me down. I wasn't able to turn my head; I believed I would never be released. When I heard my father's voice in the distance, his approaching footsteps as we crossed the street to reach the store, I knew I'd soon be freed.

Once we were inside the small store, redolent of garlic, aged cheese, salami, and sawdust, Mother sat me on top of the counter. Then she waved the envelope in my father's startled face, never looking more vibrant than at that moment, her eyes frightened yet hopeful, her lips parted.

"Ledo, Ledo," she said fervently. "It has come!"

My tall, gangly father bent over to meet the gaze of his petite and stolid wife, my mother. His expression revealed uncertainty, his large blue eyes pale and watery, like a color from a child's paint tin.

She thrust the envelope into his hand. He stared at it, slowly turning it over.

"Open it, open it," she cried out defiantly, as if she were challenging him to show his hand in a game of cards.

His long fingers shook as he cut it open with the knife he used to slice cheese.

"What is it, Ledo?" Rocco, the owner of the store, tall and husky, came over to us. His voice sounded surprisingly soft. "There are customers."

My father bowed in deference to him. "I need a moment with Rose and Eva," he said.

"Is Eva okay?" he asked in a distracted yet concerned way.

Rocco placed his thumb and strong forefinger on either side of my chin, sternly stroking it, peering into my eyes as if he were a doctor.

"Eva's fine," my father said, shaking his head. "I need a moment with Rose."

Rocco went over to the customers at the meat stand. My parents left me on the counter and went outside. Through the glass door I saw them on the street: my father in a stained white apron, the top of my mother's head level with the middle of his chest. They were talking excitedly, their hands flailing. And then suddenly Father reached out and picked her up. I leaned forward, not wanting to lose sight of her feet, which moved with the quick frantic motion of two silvery fish swimming in the sea.

Five

Stephen, mid-June

The hush of the pre-dawn hour permeates his home like the slow burn of incense. Stephen, in his navy silk robe, descends one flight of stairs, the hardwood floor cool against his bare feet as he goes to the kitchen to make a cup of tea. When he looked in on Ned moments ago, he was reassured by the contentment in his son's sleeping face. But in their bedroom, Brea had been restless in her sleep. She hasn't been herself lately—more uneasy and dissatisfied, he thinks, wondering if she's begun to smoke again. Wasn't it a whiff of tobacco he caught when she got into bed last night?

As this is his favorite time of day, he refuses to allow his concerns to intrude for too long; this is the hour in which thoughts and images pass through his mind like a series of unfinished paintings. His musings never reach any conclusions; they just linger. Then once the sun fully ascends the horizon, Stephen will settle into the day and accept what is before him.

His study, facing east, is on the first floor down the hallway past the kitchen. With a cup of tea in hand, he steps into the room and sits in the puckered leather chair next to his desk, placing the saucer on the round tiled table, raising his slippered feet onto the ottoman. Before him are four long, narrow windows, curving in a semicircle. He leans over, reaching to switch on the small reading lamp on the desk.

In this early morning time, alone in his study sipping his tea, his thoughts flow, sustain him, allow him to focus on his work for the remainder of the day.

When he looks out the window, he sees mostly darkness and his faint reflection in the glass from the glow of the lamp. He catches a glimpse of his expression, his raised eyebrows, his chin lifted, his mouth slightly opened; it is an older version of the photograph on his desk propped up unframed against the base of the lamp. In this picture, he is ten years old and his expression is earnest and open, mildly amazed; he is in a museum in Florence standing before Michelangelo's *David*. In her small, straight script, his mother had written "December/Christmas, 1968," on the back of the picture, the ink now smudged. He discovered the photograph a few years ago among his mother's belongings shortly after her death. The picture is a bit faded; his expression is what is most defined.

Although he was regarded as a solemn boy, in this photograph he appears more vulnerable, more open.

He was two years younger than Ned is now. It was the year of a presidential election. The world was a far different place then, ordered on the surface of things, yet equally chaotic. Not like things are now—hardly any order, mostly chaos. His mother had been politically active, and had campaigned tirelessly at first for Eugene McCarthy, because she'd earnestly believed he would end the war and care for the disadvantaged. She'd become another person then, the only period in her life she'd really been involved in a cause beyond her family and had shed her natural shyness.

During that time she would be away for long periods, and he would yearn for her. Stephen still remembers how he longed for her to come home as he waited in bed while she was at one political rally or another. And he'd hear voices in the night, his father talking to a colleague, he assumed, either on the phone or in person, sometimes laughter, and then silence. His burden was that zigzagging sense of apprehension so palpable in a sensitive child. Growing up, he battled with his overly responsive nature, attempting to defeat it, as David had slain Goliath. But it was age that eventually helped him put his emotions in place.

What would his mother have thought of politicians today if she were alive? he wonders. Have they really helped the disadvantaged? Stopped wars?

And there was his father too, with his dedication to his work, his constant focus on his patients. So they decided to travel to Florence, Italy, as a family for Christmas after the 1968 election. They wanted to be alone, to enjoy one another's company, to submerge themselves in art—what better place than Florence to do so, his father had said—but most importantly to forget their life back home for a while.

Did his family truly bond during that Christmas in Florence? What has taken precedence in his memory is the silence as he stood with his hands clasped behind his back before the statue of David, watching his uncharacteristically agitated father out of the corner of his eye, while his mother took the photo that leans against the lamp on his desk. He looks over at the picture, now bathed in the muted light of the half-risen sun.

His son Ned has much more opportunity to express himself than he did at ten or twelve, or at any other age for that matter; it is because of Brea, her solid presence in his life.

Because Brea rarely complains, he must take seriously her request to return to New York. Yet again he thinks how different she's been lately—especially these past two weeks.

Her voice is tense whenever she paces back and forth in her study, preparing for the role of Mrs. Alving—Ibsen's *Ghosts*—before the first rehearsal. He now hears a different kind of passion; there is a note of daring in it, almost hardness. Mrs. Alving—maybe she is connecting with this character in a deep, deep way. Mrs. Alving—isn't she conventionally unconventional, or vice versa?

Mrs. Alving . . . Mrs. Hathaway . . . he hasn't seen her since her first visit a few weeks ago—her anxiety—when he sees her again today will she understand it better?

Mrs. Hathaway. The more he thinks of it the more he realizes she doesn't bear much of a resemblance to his babysitter from his youth. Mrs. Hathaway is slender. Mrs. C.—yes, that was her name—was naturally voluptuous. Her full name was too long, too difficult to pronounce, and her bearing exuded a certain selflessness and flexibility. Mrs. Hathaway, to the contrary, is prickly—her cheekbones high like an Egyptian princess, like those sculptures of Egyptian royalty he'd gazed upon as a child at the Museum of Fine Arts, finding them both frightening and compelling.

Last night he dreamed about himself and Mrs. C. sitting on the antique yellow sofa in the living room of the Commonwealth Avenue townhouse he lived in as a child. It was a sensual dream, colorful; he recalls the velvety soft touch of the sofa. He doesn't know if he was an adult or a child in the dream. Mrs. C. said to him in a hushed voice, "Your parents are doers, not laughers." She clutched his hand, and they laughed together until it hurt—that was what had jolted him from the dream, the searing pain from the laughter. But upon waking, he found himself in tears.

Sunlight floods the study. It's time for him to get going—it's Brea's first day of rehearsal. As he stands up it comes to him, the line Brea has practiced again and again, her tone sharp and anxious, Mrs. Alving's words. Hearing uncertainty in his voice, he recites: "I thought you understood where I'd lost what you call my heart at the time."

Eva's Journal

Dr. Forester wasn't interested in what was in the letter to my father; he wanted to know what I recalled about falling off the counter. He appeared tired, worried, his eyes glazed behind his glasses. Despite the beginning of a summer tan, he looked older than he did at our first meeting.

When I sat down and faced him I pointedly told him I had no interest in keeping a journal to write about my dreams. "I want to write about what is real," I said, my voice shaky with emotion.

He uncrossed his legs and then crossed them again without losing my gaze. I'd piqued his interest. Yet he appeared not at all surprised or distracted by my unease. Had he not noticed, or had he chosen to ignore my distress?

When he asked what subject I'd decided upon, I told him I had written about my earliest memory. He said it was my prerogative whether or not I wanted to share this with him, as it was my private journal. He didn't need to see it, or hear about it.

I said I did want to discuss what I'd written because there was only so much I was able to remember. Then I recounted to him my recollection of my mother carrying me in her arms on that cold November day, and that she'd had a letter she was bringing to my father at the store where he worked. I explained how I recalled this day in a series of flashes. And by writing the moments I remembered, the flashes had come together, connecting.

His eyes widened when I told him I'd been left on the counter while my parents went outside to talk privately about the letter, and that I'd been left alone with Rocco, my father's boss. Then I described the last and clearest memory I have of that day—the movement of my mother's feet, like small fish swimming in the sea.

He asked me if I recalled what I felt at that moment. I told him the memory was very hazy, but what I was most certain about was that I'd experienced a sense of deep solace watching my mother's feet as my father lifted her in the air.

Was I frightened of Rocco, my father's employer? he asked. An image of Rocco, large and smiling, wearing the smell of garlic like cologne, crossed my mind. I felt emotional, yet I shrugged and said I didn't know if I had been fearful of Rocco. I was so young I only vaguely knew his name was Rocco.

I told Dr. Forester it was my father's older sister, my aunt Lora, who years later told me that I'd fallen off the counter, and had an awful bruise on my forehead that lasted for a long while. They left me alone because they were so excited about the letter, preoccupied by it, I said. I added that it was understandable, as that letter changed our life.

But as I said, Dr. Forester wasn't interested in the letter. He wanted to know how I felt years later when I learned I'd gotten a terrible bruise on my forehead. Had I been surprised by this information? Disconcerted?

He appeared to move in his seat when asking these questions, but it was so subtle, like a sigh; I didn't know if he had, or if it was my imagination.

"I was shocked," I answered readily, impatiently. "They were always so careful with me, that it didn't seem like something they'd do—leave me alone on a counter at such a young age. In fact," I said, "they were generally overly protective of me throughout my childhood, embarrassingly so. They usually wanted Aunt Lora around to help them take care of me. So I was often with three adults."

"Because of your aunt Lora's presence—is that why you found them to be overly protective?" he asked. "Were they as doting and careful with you when she wasn't around?"

"Are you asking me if I believe they felt guilty, and were trying to compensate for the rest of my childhood by having Aunt Lora help them?" I asked, my words rushing together.

"Yes and no," he said. "I am more interested in your interpretation of what happened—even more than whatever memory you may retain of that day."

"Well, I've always thought about it in terms of the letter," I said. "I forgave them because of what was in the letter. It seemed . . . ," I began. I stopped suddenly and said to him, "You are frustrating me; I want to tell

31

you about the letter. I need to tell you about the letter. That will explain everything."

"Because it changed your life?" he asked.

"Of course," I answered, angry.

"And that was more important than your bruise?"

"Accidents happen," I said firmly, staring into his cat-like eyes. Then I stood up, told him I was leaving.

"Would you like to schedule another appointment?" he asked impassively.

Walking toward the door, I said, "I'll call if I do," my voice and legs shaky now because of my rage.

Six

Over the recent nights, Brea's dreams have been for the most part tranquil, hopeful, only occasionally and ever so briefly sharp, yet once her eyes open she carries no memory of them; what greets her is anxiety—startlingly palpable—as if it's hovering over her, waiting to confront her.

There are reasons for her angst, she admits. As she sits up in bed, she glances at the framed photo on the bureau of her and Stephen at a restaurant in Paris, taken two years ago. Were they as happy as they look? Brea wonders, feeling a passing sense of loss.

But most importantly, she thinks, it's the first day of rehearsal for *Ghosts*, and she's always hesitant and uneasy when she takes on a new part. She invariably feels as exposed and as uncertain as she was when she auditioned for her first off-Broadway role all those years ago; how the theater lights shone down on her harshly, as if she were under interrogation, and how she had to battle to maintain her composure.

Today, as always, her challenge is to interpret in a unique way the character she will be playing. Brea has never before taken on the role of Mrs. Alving; she finds her to be a most complicated character. Flexible? Strong? Distracted? How to portray her? How does Mrs. Alving stand? Sit? Speak? Suffer? And what are the ghosts? Old ideas and beliefs? Her failings? Flaws of loved ones? Brea smiles thoughtfully.

Ever since she was young she has possessed an awareness and acceptance of human imperfections. "Uncanny—for someone of your age," her mother would say in her no-nonsense voice whenever a nine-, ten-, or eleven-year-old Brea would gently reproach her for criticizing a friend or relative, reminding her mother that no one ever always does the right thing.

While in college studying theater, Brea expected a certain amount of disharmony with her classmates or professors—accepting any strife that might occur as being natural. She'd always been grounded—lambently so—possessing a strong sense of reality, never over-bearing, more lighthearted. This was partly because of her temperament, along with her discovery at a young age that those closest to her had failings, which in turn invariably caused her to realize her own.

Brea tosses aside the white comforter and runs her hand over Stephen's side of the bed. He's at the gym, she thinks, and hopes he'll be back before she leaves for the theater. Her angst this morning, she realizes, is mostly because of Peter Sands. Their affair all those years ago had unnerved her so that at the time she

had considered giving up acting. It isn't really sur-
prising she and Peter will be crossing paths again—
Sam having hired Peter to play the role of Pastor
Manders—it was bound to occur one day or another;
theater people move around, especially on the East
Coast.

She had known Peter when she was twenty-five—a
girl really! What does one know of life at that age? He
was twenty years her senior, and so from the start it
wasn't a healthy relationship. Her intuition had
warned her about him, but at the same time compelled
her to yield to him. But as she now perceives, it was
more about her, about what she'd been seeking, than
about him.

When she met him, Peter was playing the lead role
and she a small part in a contemporary, experimental
play that had lasted for a short time off Broadway. At
first she strongly disliked Peter, his arrogance, his
sleek blond hair. Then one day Peter approached her
and asked her to have a drink with him after the play.
She hadn't yet removed her makeup, and he touched
the side of her face with his hand, the white smearing
his fingers, and as finicky as he was, it hadn't bothered him. "Brea," he said, "it rhymes with free." She
hadn't refused him, as that wasn't her style; she didn't
like cutting people off, not even the arrogant ones.

She now gets out of bed, puts on her robe, goes
over to the window and pulls up the blinds, feeling
invigorated by the caressing sunlight. She opens the
window. The warmth of the sun covers her neck and
chest. Peter had taught her things, she recalls, whet-
ting her appetite, so to speak. And after her time with
him, she'd sought out men like him, that is, until she

met Stephen—he didn't possess the same feral nature as Peter and the others. He was different—he wanted love. And she was determined to suppress the hard, edgy side of herself Peter had uncovered.

She never told Stephen about Peter, because he really wasn't interested in her past affairs, and neither was she in his—it was all a growing process, he'd said to her once, when she began to tell him about someone she'd been intimate with for a few years. "We're not now what we were in the past, though the past follows us a little, but we're always moving forward; we must outrun it a bit," he'd said matter-of-factly.

She prefers how Stephen thinks, so unusual, so out of the norm, rarely conventional, straightforward and complex at the same time—it's the way she tries to approach the characters she plays. All her past lovers, theater people mostly, were really at heart much more conventional than Stephen. And Peter Sands was as conventional as all the others; he'd just had a stronger hold on her.

When Sam called ten days ago to tell her Peter would be playing the part of Pastor Manders, it was as if she'd been stung. "I understand you know him. He said he's worked with you before. That's encouraging. Maybe there'll be good chemistry between the two of you, and that should help the play," Sam had said, his voice impartial.

Sam is intrinsically a cynical man, she thinks, feeling mildly drawn to him. Is he intending to use whatever he knows about her and Peter to manipulate them? Manipulate her performance?

As she is about to step into the shower she unexpectedly hears strains of "Für Elise." She turns, and goes to pick up her cell phone from the top of the bureau. When she sees who it is, she answers it and says, "It's awfully early to be calling, Sam."

He ignores her words, and bluntly tells her that Peter has broken his foot playing tennis, and so he's had to cancel. He will not be mobile enough to be in the play.

Then before hanging up, Sam says abruptly, "I'll take his place. I'll play Manders."

Brea throws the phone on the comforter. No Peter, she thinks, surprised she's disappointed. As she turns on the hot water knob in the shower, she considers Sam in the role of Pastor Manders. She takes a deep breath to calm herself. The steam now rising, she anxiously cries out, "I thought you understood where I'd lost what you call my heart at the time!"

Eva's Journal

My parents referred to the letter as their redemption. I was never quite certain what they meant—who was redeeming whom; though I believe it may have had to do with their feeling of acceptance once they received the news. The letter changed our lives because my father was now able to realize his dream, and my mother hers. Because she deeply appreciated music and my father's talent, it took some time for me realize her longings were of a more practical nature.

How could Dr. Forester interpret an accident like mine—falling off a counter—as anything other than an innocent mishap? An opportunity such as this was not easy or common, and so they'd become preoccupied with the letter.

Two weeks earlier my father had auditioned at a nightclub in Boston called Happenings. With the letter came a contract for his services as a jazz pianist.

How tightly I clutched my mother's hand the first night he played at Happenings. It was so dark; all I could clearly see was the round stage.

When my father went up to the piano, he brushed his hand across the top of the shiny black surface, appearing ill at ease. The owner came over to him and slapped his back. "It will go well tonight, Ledo, it will go well," he said in a jovial voice.

Mother looked frightened. We stood at the back of the room. I tugged at her hand, wanting to go home. But she didn't move, ignoring my desire to leave.

Closely I watched as Father sat down at the piano, spreading out his fingers, touching the keys gingerly, not making a sound. He took a deep breath, his shoulders forward, and then his fingers firmly struck the keys. Music flooded the room. When Mother bent down to hug me, her eyes were filled with tears.

Seven

Stephen, mid-June

A Saturday morning and Stephen, at his desk in his study, is starting work on the lecture he'll be giving in Florence. As he reaches over to switch on the lamp, his arm brushes the photo of himself as a young boy in front of Michelangelo's *David*, and it slides down onto the desk. When he picks it up and leans it against the lamp, he is struck by how erect his posture is in the picture. An image crosses his mind of that young child standing ever so straight, banging on the front door of the woman's dress shop on that misty night some weeks ago. The boy must have been about the same age he was in this photo.

Hazily Stephen remembers going with a woman into a clothing store on Newbury Street on a cool fall day, standing beside her, resting his chin on top of the counter as she purchased a brown sweater dress. Yet he's not able to recall who she was.

No sense racking my brain, he thinks, and begins to work on his lecture. Soon his study is filled with sunlight, and he switches off the lamp. When he gets up to close the blinds so he can better read the computer screen, he notices a copy of Brea's script on the chair next to the window. He picks it up, smiling. She wants him to read *Ghosts* before he sees the play and has left it there for him as a reminder. Invariably he reads the script before going to one of her performances. But not the first time he saw her act.

And wasn't Brea wearing a brown dress that night? She played the energetic Gwendolen in an off-Broadway production of *The Importance of Being Earnest*. And her dress was long and sweeping, and yes, brown. As he watched her, his laughter had been intense, heartfelt, aching over how she delivered her lines in a quick, lively way, her eyes darting. Yet when he got to know her he realized she wasn't very restive; in fact, she was careful and warm, occasionally edgy, perhaps closer to the character of the romantic and understanding Cecily. "Brea," he says her name as if it rhymes with Leah—two syllables.

As he waited for her at the stage door exit after the play was over, he held the program close and read her name again and again. A light snow fell, dissolving on the pavement.

"You're the first person who's ever pronounced it that way," she said when he called out to her.

"Coffee, would you like to have coffee?" he responded. Never before had he pursued an actress—or anyone, really—but because there had been something so compelling about her, he'd been unable to stop himself. He hadn't slept the two previous nights; there had been so many emergencies at the hospital. And so he was exhausted.

"Coffee," she repeated, tilting her head as if she were assessing him yet preoccupied with other thoughts at the same time. "I don't know you."

But he could tell by the subtle movement in her lips that she was intrigued.

"Are you a doctor?" she asked, gazing at his chest. He realized that in his rush to get to the theater on time, he had neglected to put on a shirt over his scrubs. Immediately he sensed her pragmatism, mild though it might be. It was there in a bright and comforting way, and he felt reassured.

He nodded. Without saying any more to one another, they began to stroll in the same direction. He noticed her shiver and then turn up the collar of her coat.

"I was involved with a doctor once, a few years ago, a cardiologist," she said. "It didn't end very well." She pressed her lips together, as if she was uncertain whether or not to say more.

She stopped walking, turned towards him decisively. "What's your name?"

At that moment he knew she'd chosen in his favor, and he was hopeful.

"You're smiling," she said softly, after he'd introduced himself.

"You aren't running away," he answered in his wistful, wry way.

He could tell she liked his response by the way she lifted her chin and said directly, "I've always made it a point to be open-minded."

They both laughed as they entered the coffee shop, eager to get out of the snow, falling more heavily now.

What Stephen remembers most about that conversation, which lasted until two in the morning, were her expressions, how she bit her lower lip when she spoke about her parents' divorce, her oval-shaped face appearing more angular. How she looked younger, her eyes brightening when she spoke about her love of the theater and how she'd made the decision to become an actress. She could never sleep the night before an audition, especially if it was for a part she so desperately wanted. When she spoke about the dark side of theater life, the pettiness, the efforts people made to appear different, to stand out, she appeared older. And it was at that moment he fell in love with her, when he knew he couldn't leave her. It was her maturity and naïvety bundled together.

And when it was his turn to talk, he knew he sounded ponderous as he haltingly explained his life up to that point, his disappointments, his successes, his admiration for his father, who had passed away six months before—an extreme admiration at times, but very real. He told her how his mother had transformed herself from a housewife to a political activist, and had had an affair that had cut him deeply, affecting his life and his ability to trust. "I hated her deception," he said, almost too intently. His father had been stoic, too forgiving. He was eight or so when it all started, but he hadn't found out about the affair until later. Because of his mother's deception things had never been easy for him with women. He'd had his disillusionments like others. But he blamed himself for his insecurities.

Because of his discomfort about what he was revealing so easily, so effortlessly, from time to time he'd cease talking, not wanting to say more. To this day he feels shaken whenever he thinks of that first conversation, not because he's chagrined by what he said, but because he could so easily have turned her off with his vehemence. He'd been emotionally lost—his father's recent death.

Brea could have refused to see him again, slipped back into the dark New York night, he now thinks as he looks out his study window, sees that the rosebushes on the front lawn are in bloom. Then he crosses his legs and lowers his eyes to the script; before he begins to read, he wonders fleetingly who the woman was who had purchased the brown sweater dress.

Eva's Journal

According to Aunt Lora, Father possessed an uncanny ear for music. For at first he taught himself to play the piano.

At sixteen he left high school to work as a janitor at a community center outside of Boston. Once the other janitors left to go home, he sat at the piano in the auditorium, his head slightly tilted, his ear leading the way as he played a piece he recently heard on the radio. His fingers were long and flexible, and he moved them with rapidity and ease.

His friends urged him to perform at parties. He developed a particular rhythm, seductive, because it caught the listener by surprise at nearly every stanza. It had a stop-start, or start-stop quality to it, and you never knew when he'd be stopping or starting. Eventually it was known as "Ledo's Beat." But my father, Ledo Morelli, was anything but seductive; he was tall and gangly, with a hawk-like nose, watery eyes, and a distant, dreamy expression.

After working as a janitor for a few years, he saved enough money to take piano lessons from a young woman, a recent graduate of a music conservatory in Boston. His teacher soon realized the extent of his ability. She was from the Midwest, and had taken an apartment in the neighborhood where Father lived. She was petite and lively, with thick dark hair that fell to her waist, overpowering her body. "Ledo," she said, pressing his hand, looking up at him, "you have a talent you must pursue." Her expression glowed.

Mother took piano lessons from the same music teacher. After her lesson was over she organized sheet music for the teacher in an open closet in the next room while listening to my father play. My mother wasn't as gifted as he was, but she had a strong appreciation of music and was acutely aware of his talent.

Aunt Lora's recounting of how my parents met ended with the letter, and my falling off the counter and getting that bruise. She shook her head in disbelief. A rather harsh ending to a promising story, she said, and shrugged. Then she slightly tilted her head, pressed her hand to her raised cheek; she resembled a figure in a Modigliani painting. And I knew after all this time she was still unnerved by the accident.

I was eleven when she told me about the bruise. Father's playing now fully supported us. On most nights he performed at Happenings. But two weekends a month he played in New York, at a club on Fifty-Fourth Street. Mother would accompany him and I'd stay behind with Aunt Lora and her husband.

I had an exaggerated sense of my father's success, and an imaginative accomplice in Aunt Lora, who encouraged me see my parents' life in an idealized way. But eventually I would discover I was more practical than my aunt, that my understanding of life was much different from hers—though I didn't realize this until I was in my late teens and early twenties.

She was my father's older and only sibling, and her appearance was more stunning than beautiful. Her husband worked as a courier in Boston, and she was employed as a part-time clerk at Woolworth's on Main Street. Every afternoon after work, she'd come to our home.

Because she and her husband were childless, she focused much of her attention on me. My active mother easily accepted the close relationship I had with my aunt, who appeared as if she were overwhelmed by the amount of free time she had.

But in the company of her husband, Aunt Lora was quiet and restrained. She'd sit next to him with her legs crossed, her head down, seeming to concentrate on his words. Or she'd go and sit alone in the next room. He was too serious—so opposite from her that it bothered me. And whenever Uncle Mario said my name, I was uneasy. He called me Eve, as if he had someone else in mind.

He was as well groomed as Aunt Lora, but their styles were different; he wore mostly dark clothes, close-fitted, and she dressed in light-colored flowing blouses and skirts. She was well proportioned, and he was slight. Because she wasn't her natural self when she was with her husband, I distrusted him. He angered me. He was as solemn and obdurate as she was light and ardent.

Yet whenever Aunt Lora came up the front steps of our home, she moved in a slow, languid way, a distracted look in her eyes. But once I opened the door, her expression was warm and intense. She leaned forward and robustly kissed my forehead. She was so many things at once.

Eight

Brea and Stephen, mid-June

Out on the deck at the back of their home, Stephen and Brea are sitting at a wicker table beneath a white-and-blue striped umbrella, having lunch. Brea's lilac skirt and top, Stephen notices, are a few shades lighter than the color of the trim of the house. And it occurs to him she's been more attentive to color lately, whether it be in her choice of clothes or in her recent attempt to redecorate their home. He finds this change in her perplexing, as she's never been particularly exacting about her appearance or their furnishings.

The noon sun is strong. Suddenly warm, Stephen takes off the jacket of his gray seersucker suit.

"Stephen, I've been thinking about things," she says in a pressured voice.

The sound of a landscaper mowing a neighbor's lawn is distant, muted.

"What things?"

"The twists and turns our lives have taken."

"I believe our life together has been pretty smooth, if you think about it," he says, hearing a certain arrogance in his voice. "We've been together for fourteen years—it really isn't that long of a time."

"Yes, but Stephen, we are no longer young," she says emphatically, and sets down what is left of the sandwich she's mostly eaten.

"Neither are we old."

He studies Brea and thinks of his mother, who he'd seen only nibble at her food, how so very different she'd been than Brea, how much more expansive and expressive Brea is—his mother had been small, composed, yet emotionally scattered, loving in a staccato-like way.

When Brea looks up, he catches her gaze.

"How was rehearsal this morning? Is the casting going smoothly?" he asks, still silently comparing and contrasting the two women.

"Wish it were going better," she says evenly.

"What's wrong?"

"It's not easy," she says.

He nods, his heart thumping. "Nothing is, Brea."

"Do you mean our life together hasn't been easy?"

"I think we get along better than most," he says and takes a sip from the glass of lemonade, surprised to see his hand shake.

"Stephen, you'll never completely understand why I want to live in New York again—never!" she cries out, suddenly angry.

She stands up, picks up her plate. Sharply opens the sliding glass door that separates the kitchen from the deck, and disappears inside. Alone at the table, Stephen looks up at the sky, a very pale blue, almost turquoise, and wonders what she isn't telling him about the play.

Through the opening in the sliding glass door, he sees Brea in the kitchen, one hand on her hip, talking on her cell phone, and he's suddenly disgruntled— Brea, who's always been straightforward, isn't so any more. Is she really any different from his mother? He experiences the same uncertainty he'd felt when he was young, not knowing if his mother would be home that night, or a few nights later. Even when he was older, he'd always felt unsure about her thoughts, her whereabouts.

And then there was that night when he was about fifteen and he had come unannounced into the living room. As he approached, the crackling fire was the only sound he heard, and so he was surprised to see his mother seated in the antique yellow armchair, dressed in a coral-colored dress that fell past her knees, her ankles crossed, her light red, shoulder-length hair loose and wavy. She leaned towards Philip Barone, once a student of his father's, now a senior fellow, who sat on the sofa across from her. Her expression was soft, yielding, her eyes small, nearly closed, a strand of hair falling across her cheek.

Philip, dressed in chinos and a blue collared shirt, no tie, leaned toward her as if to better hear her soft and thoughtful words. The light from the lamp caught the hem of his mother's skirt and the cuff of Philip's pants, bonding them together in Stephen's mind in some way. For the first time, Stephen realized that

Philip found his mother intriguing, that they were mildly attracted to one another.

Now as he looks across the street he sees a young boy swinging a bat in his front yard, reminding him that Philip had spoken about the Red Sox that evening, a subject his father had no interest in; he'd only gone to one of Stephen's games. Baseball was too literal for his taste, he'd told Stephen, though he encouraged him to continue playing if that was what he enjoyed. "Never shy away from what pleases you and at the same time provides you with a sense of accomplishment," he'd said to his son.

Once Stephen's father arrived, Philip's demeanor changed; he became almost as serious and as energetic as Arthur Forester. When his father greeted Philip, Stephen noticed an expression of regret in his mother's pale eyes as though she knew the conversation would now focus on Arthur, Arthur's latest writings, and Arthur's admiration of Philip. Stephen always found his father to be an imposing figure; he believed and maybe even feared that at any moment he might do the unexpected.

As they sat at the table, Philip to Arthur's right, Stephen to his left, Arthur picked up his fork and looked directly at Philip. "Philip," he asked, "what do you think of my latest paper on the divided self?"

Stephen, looking over at his mother, saw that her eyes were now closed. He noticed Philip quietly studying her before responding. At the head of the table, Arthur easily cut into his piece of roast, his long, thin fingers looking bereft and pale without rings.

Philip hesitated, blushing slightly. "I agree with you, Dr. Forester. The divided inner self working in opposition to itself is not necessarily pejorative or deviant in all cases."

Arthur smiled broadly. "Yes, Philip—that is my point," he said, waving his knife, as if it were a sword he was deftly brandishing. "If understood correctly, the divided self ultimately enhances the personality."

That night Stephen had knocked on the door of his parents' bedroom. His head throbbed. A muffled voice—his mother's—told him to come in. When he opened the door, he saw she was in her nightgown, sitting at the edge of the bed, her hair tightly pulled back with a rubber band, her eyes filled with tears. His father was at the window in his silk robe, looking out at the dark Boston night, tilting his head in the direction of Arlington Street and the entrance of the Public Gardens where the statue of George Washington stood. At this time of night, it must be encircled by the city lights, Stephen thought. And despite his headache, he was hopeful.

But when Stephen looked over at his mother, he gasped; he wasn't certain if it was a shadow or a bruise across her upper arm. He put his hand over his forehead. His mother, drawing on her robe, came over to him. In a subdued voice, she asked Arthur to find some pills to help Stephen's migraine go away.

Moments later, nearly forgetting his headache, he turned and left the quiet room, believing what he'd seen on his mother's arm had been a shadow.

Yes, Philip, he thinks, now his mentor and colleague. For some reason, despite Philip's apparent interest in his mother all those years ago, Stephen had trusted him.

As he looks again through the glass door and sees Brea still on the phone, now gesticulating, he thinks about his mother's arm that night, and then Eva Hathaway's bruise. He feels an ache in his chest. Why had his mother not been more of a presence in his life, more forthcoming about her own? And now Brea? He gets up, deciding he'll confront her.

Eva's Journal

On the nights I went to Happenings and wasn't sleepy, didn't need to rest on the sofa in the back, I sat on velvet pillows in the coat room with a woman named Claudia. Claudia was responsible for checking in women's mink stoles and fur jackets. She was small, with short dark hair and a pointy nose, businesslike, but from time to time she'd glance at me without meeting my gaze and ask quick sharp questions about school and my family. I was careful to sit up straight, and I answered her questions softly while listening to Father play, his music seeming to come from a far distance.

One night I wasn't feeling well. Aunt Lora stayed with me while Mother and Father were at the nightclub. I was ten at the time. Aunt Lora's husband never came with her when she took care of me at my home. I'd gone to bed early, and I remember being awakened by the sound of Aunt Lora crying. She was speaking to Uncle

Mario over the phone. With much anguish she called out his name. I got out of bed and went to her. When she noticed me, she wiped her tears and told Uncle Mario she had to get off the phone and tend to me.

Sadly she lowered her head to meet my gaze, her large hazel eyes glazed and watery. But her mood didn't last for long. Suddenly she grinned, then winked and said, "I am silly, Eva—so silly to cry," but her voice, hoarse and frail, betrayed her melancholy.

Eventually I forgot that she'd been crying. That's how it was with Aunt Lora—she helped you forget not only your own sadness, but hers as well. When I was with her I'd forget how difficult it was for me to find a good friend at school. People in our small city thought our life was odd because my father was a musician. When I was with Aunt Lora, all those worries disappeared. But on that night, after she left, I lay sleepless in bed. For now I was concerned about her.

The next day I asked Aunt Lora why she never went to Happenings. I knew she enjoyed music. When we spent time together, she'd often turn on the radio, and in her sultry way she'd sway to the beat of the music. But instead of answering my question, she hugged me. I remember being overwhelmed by the scent of her perfume.

When I approached Mother, her face reddened, and she said in that quick way of hers that Aunt Lora used to come to Happenings, and then she just stopped. I never asked my father why Aunt Lora didn't go to the nightclub, as I knew he would not answer me directly.

I felt partly sorry for Aunt Lora, as her life consisted of going from her home to the Woolworth's store, and then to visit us. But she'd always dress as if she were going to a place of much importance—clothes of the finest quality, and shoes and a handbag matching her outfit—she deserved a more sophisticated life, I believed.

For me, Aunt Lora was separate from Happenings and Father's piano playing, but at the same time she was an essential person in my life. It was as if my childhood had two distinct parts to it—one with my father and my mother and my time at Happenings, and the other with Aunt Lora, who was my guide not only to my present life, but also to my mother and father's life before I was born. I don't know if she was particularly fond of my parents, but she was loyal to them, as an older sister is to younger siblings. For my mother was the sister she never had. And so I would go back and forth between Mother and Father's world and the world of Aunt Lora, as she went back and forth between taking care of me and living with her dark and intense husband.

The world of Mother and Father and Happenings was smoky, edgy, and tiring, while my time with Aunt Lora was as comforting and as imaginative as she was. Yet eventually I would discover neither my parents nor Aunt Lora were the people I had thought them to be.

Nine

Stephen, late June

He hears a steady knock on the outer office door, which he locked after his last patient of the day left twenty minutes ago. He checks his watch; it's a little past six.

Brea stands there looking a bit tired in the eyes, her shoulders not as erect as usual. He kisses her quickly, instinctively, thinking of how she'd adamantly denied she was keeping something from him when he'd confronted her a few weeks ago.

"Late rehearsal?" he asks.

She nods, and sits down in a chair in the waiting room across from the copy of the Van Gogh painting. There's a plopping sound from the pump in the tank and the fish now frenetically move about.

"Too tired to talk?" he asks abruptly, then returns to his office. Soon he calls out, "I'm almost done. Where's Ned?"

"At a friend's for the night," she says quietly.

"Let's go out to dinner," he suggests, trying to sound more amiable but uneasy after having been curt with her. For she only occasionally comes up to his office and rarely sits in his waiting room.

She looks up at him as he stands in the doorway. Not meeting his gaze, she points to the copy of the Van Gogh painting. "Do you remember when you went to the conference in Ohio? Was it two years ago? Where you'd seen the original at the Cincinnati Art Museum?"

He nods, feeling slightly chagrinned.

"You were restless when you came home—I'd never really seen that side of you before. At dinner you rapped your fist on the table and said that you must hire an artist to make a copy of the painting, that you wanted if for your waiting room. And later that night in bed I'd been overwhelmed; you were so different."

His heart beating rapidly, he moves toward her. She gets up from the chair. "The figures look shaky," she says, pointing again to the copy of the Van Gogh. "Do you see us in that painting, Stephen?" she asks directly.

"Part of us," he says, turning to study the Van Gogh copy.

Disquieted, they walk toward the restaurant. It is a warm summer evening; the sun has not yet set. They are silent, their shoulders touching from time to time. Stephen notices a woman in the distance, going into the convenience store on the corner. And he feels a wave of recognition, before realizing it might have been Mrs. Hathaway. He smiles as he remembers her leaving his office in anger. If only she knew how often this happens with patients, he thinks. And they usually do come back, but sometimes they don't.

Brea grasps his arm, stopping him in his tracks.

"Stephen, here it is. You were about to pass the restaurant."

They enter the dark wood foyer, and the hostess immediately recognizes them, escorts them to a table with a view of the ocean. The restaurant isn't crowded, but there's a buzz of conversation about the room.

As they eat, he tells Brea that Philip Barone and his wife will not be coming to Florence this summer. "He called today to apologize. He won't be there for my talk," he says, shrugging.

Brea eyes light up. "I like Philip," she says. "That's nice of him to apologize. I don't know what to make of his wife though; she's too quiet, but seems kind enough."

"Shy, I suppose," Stephen answers, protective of Philip's wife.

Brea half smiles, then places her hand over his. "Stephen, have you thought more about moving back to New York?" Her voice grows tense.

He doesn't know what to say. It crosses his mind that she's tired of their marriage.

"To be honest, no, I haven't. But I wonder if you're right about thinking we could live there again. We're settled here. Moving Ned out of school and away from his friends so suddenly—I don't know about that. And my practice—I have obligations, professional obligations."

She rests her chin on her curled hand, her eyes half-closed.

"Is it so bad here, Brea?"

"I don't know if it's Harrington, or me, or something else. I'm tired all the time now, not physically—I'm mentally tired, maybe emotionally."

"How did rehearsal go today?" he asks cautiously, knowing what a perfectionist she is, wondering if she's simply discouraged after a long day.

"Okay. I'm not used to Sam acting and directing at the same time—it's jarring."

"How is his acting?"

"Not as intrusive as his directing—in fact, better."

"That's a good sign, isn't it? Though I imagine it must be more difficult for you to play your role when he's both acting and directing."

"Yes."

"So, is that why you want to return to New York?"

"Are you asking if Sam is getting under my skin, so much so that I need to be away from him?"

"I suppose I am. But Brea, you're much more focused than he is. You need to stay with it until the end of the summer—you've made a commitment and it isn't like you to break one. And once it's over, you can decide. You could commute back and forth to New York for a while, and then we all could move there, eventually."

"Thanks, you're kind, Stephen. I didn't think you'd understand my need to go back to New York, but I believe you do," she says earnestly.

There's a knot in his throat as he wonders why she's stayed with him. They're so different. Compatible? We haven't given up trying to be, he thinks.

"Do you think it's you and not Sam who's unsettling me?" She asks this in a teasing voice. "Despite all your professional experience, you don't know me, or us, very well."

"You win, Brea," he says and smiles.

She grows serious again. "About New York, Stephen—I agree with you. I don't want to break the commitment I've made to play Mrs. Alving this summer. It's challenging—she's a complex character. And there's so much I can learn, even though Sam is getting in the way, day in and day out. I'll do my best." She sighs. "In the fall, I'll see what I can drum up in New York—go to some auditions—stay with Mother for a day or two—yes, I'll commute. Ned will be a teenager. He won't need me to be around as much. He's ready for some independence." She smiles. "Yes, Stephen, that is what I'll do."

As they stroll back to his office after dinner, he says, "Let's think about our trip to Florence in late August. That will help us get through the summer."

"Yes, Florence," she says, eagerly grasping his hand. "I saw that picture on your desk the other day, you in front of Michelangelo's *David*. How old were you? I don't think I've seen that one before."

"I found it among Mother's belongings; I put it aside, and came across it again about a month or so ago. Mother took the photograph. I decided to put it on my desk. I should frame it."

"Yes, Stephen, I like it. You look earnest, expectant, your whole life before you. I'm surprised the museum guards allowed her to take a picture."

"In a subtle way, I suppose, Mother had a crafty side to her," he says, and thinks how it was her silence in certain instances that was more confounding than any action she might have taken.

When they reach the office parking lot, Stephen tells her go on ahead; he'll be home in fifteen minutes or so. He wants to check his messages. As he walks towards his office, he looks across the square at the women's clothing shop, thinks of the child he saw that misty night, remembers being in a clothing store with a woman, and now recalls standing alone just outside the dressing room door while she tried on the brown dress.

Moments later he looks out his office window, watching as Brea drives away. He recalls how nearly fifteen years ago she'd stood at the front exit of the theater, looking for him, her eyes glistening. He saw her before she noticed him and so he savored that moment, hoping it wasn't only her performance she was happy about. It was the night after they'd first met. He regretted not having gone again to the play that evening. She was wearing a dark green coat and large onyx earrings.

He waved, but doesn't remember what he said to her. He only knows he felt incredibly light and happy, despite the long day at the hospital, relieved that he'd unburdened himself the previous night. He wouldn't talk about such serious things tonight. He could be free now that he'd told her so much.

When she finally saw Stephen, she smiled radiantly and went over to him; taking his arm, she immediately told him the performance had gone well, and that she was giddy with pride.

Over dinner they discussed writers they liked, operas they preferred, musicians. They both favored classical music. He liked the precision of Mozart; she liked Beethoven's passion and Liszt too—the Hungarian Rhapsodies—Liszt was wonderfully romantic, yet deep, not fluffy, she said defiantly. Not fluffy at all, she repeated, her expression becoming anguished. And then she covered her face with her hands.

Stephen hears the steady tick of the clock on the wall. Brea's anguish, he thinks angrily—her anguish then, her anguish now—she's like a chameleon. One minute she's ebullient, the next apparently in conflict about something—is she forever acting out one role or another?

He goes over to the telephone and plays his messages. Soon he hears Mrs. Hathaway's warm and gravelly voice. His heartbeat quickens.

"I've decided to come and see you again, Doctor."

Ten

Brea, late June

B rea, driving home alone, feels a light breeze on her neck, tickling her spine, chilling her spirits. It has grown dark, and there are very few street lights.

She wasn't completely honest with Stephen tonight. Yes, Sam is intrusive, but she's used to his intrusiveness, his point-blank directing style, and in terms of his acting she's been quite surprised. He's a much better actor than she would have ever imagined. But what she finds most disconcerting is the character of Mrs. Alving—she can't seem to get a grip on her. She's had challenging roles before, but this one is different; this character is elusive!

At dinner she didn't tell Stephen how very difficult this role is for her. But she wonders now if he knows, and hasn't let on. They don't interfere with each other's work, other than to encourage—Stephen doting on her before the start of rehearsals and on opening night, and she, reading and praising a paper he'll present at a conference.

But right now she needs more than encouragement. She needs a new technique—a different approach— that may be the better way of expressing it, she thinks. This isn't something she can discuss with Sam either. Their styles and interpretations are different. Inwardly she's annoyed whenever she hears him explain how to take apart a character, starting with the basics—what does Mrs. Alving think about when she gets up every morning? What does she eat? How well does she sleep? That might just confuse her more—no, Sam isn't the answer. Call Peter, she thinks. He's played Pastor Manders a few times, and he might have a good read on Mrs. Alving. But that could be dicey. He'll think she's propositioning him, or he may be aloof, still carrying a grudge because of their past relationship. In her experience, some men forget, but others don't. As for her, she's always believed in letting bygones be bygones—never looking back, only looking forward.

She drives into the parking lot of the twenty-four hour convenience store. She needs to pick up some milk. Stephen won't be home for another half hour. He always lingers longer in the office than he says he will.

When she gets out of the car, she feels the breeze is much cooler now, and regrets not having brought a sweater. It's still June, she reminds herself. In New England, you are never safely into summer until July.

Inside the store she sees a woman at the check-out counter purchasing a package of cigarettes and feels a tightening in her throat. She's started smoking again, not very much of course—a cigarette here and there—

and Stephen hasn't noticed. She thinks of Peter, how they would share a cigarette, even when they knew it could harm their voices—they had found it thrilling, the risk of it all—and she feels a yearning.

When she leaves the store, she notices the woman who bought the cigarettes, outside, smoking. She's older than Brea originally thought—the fluorescent lights beneath the outside awning reveal the lines etched on her face. She is tall and slim and dressed in a tan silk skirt and cream-colored blouse; her hair reaches her shoulders. Beautiful, Brea thinks, and is struck by the image of the woman smoking a cigarette. Mrs. Alving. Is there something about her, her intensity? Mrs. Alving is essentially a conflicted character; her inner struggles are what make her beautiful— perhaps just like this woman.

The woman nods at her, and Brea, forgetting about her craving for a cigarette, returns her smile.

The woman snuffs out her cigarette with the toe of her shoe, and goes over to a car. Before she gets in, she turns and looks straight at Brea. "You're Doctor Forester's wife, aren't you?" she asks.

Brea is startled. The woman's voice has unnerved her; it gives the impression she wants you to think she knows something you don't.

Brea nods and hurries over to her own car, chilled now from within.

Eva's Journal

As I walked towards the convenience store this evening, I caught a glimpse of Dr. Forester. With him was his wife, I assumed. It was the dinner hour, and I guessed they were heading toward the Oceanside Restaurant at the end of the street near the wharf. I'd not seen his wife before. Though I've heard she's an actress at the Playhouse by the Sea, where she goes by the name Brea, just Brea. Bill and I have lived here for two years, but haven't yet gone to Harrington's theater. If we want to see a play, we usually drive to New York for a week-end.

Dr. Forester's wife is talented, I've heard, and when she worked in New York she used her full name. Some say—rumors, of course—that she's involved with the director of the playhouse—Sam—Wilkins, I believe, is his last name. I met him at a cocktail party when we first moved to Harrington. Bill has been involved in a project here, and Sam's wife or ex-wife is a local architect, working on the same project. Supposedly Sam and his wife aren't on intimate terms but sometimes socialize together. I'm not certain whether or not they live together—a marriage of convenience of some sort. I never question people's lives, as mine so far hasn't been one to emulate.

Seeing Dr. Forester with his wife prompted me to leave a message on his voice mail to set up another appointment. I need to say more to him, to continue this fiction or charade, because in some odd way I believe it will lead me to the truth. The truth, as I so audaciously mentioned to him during my first appointment. The truth—when I've gone to him without revealing who I am.

It's not as if my presence will ever be a consolation to Dr. Forester—quite the opposite. On days that I lose sight of my purpose, I'm uncertain of my motivation—maybe it's simply that I need to talk more. He is, after all, a psychiatrist, and I've had a pretty unusual—or more accurately, disturbing—life.

Dr. Forester appeared distracted when he was walking with his wife. He wore that distant expression I find annoying. Yet at the same time, whenever he has that look and then responds to what I've been saying, I realize he wasn't as inattentive as I believed. But this evening he was with his wife, not one of his patients, and I wondered what was on his mind.

There was something about his expression that encouraged me to call and ask for another appointment. Maybe it was longing on my part, a yearning for the past, or perhaps it was simply anger. I don't know.

Later in the evening, I saw his wife again. I'd forgotten to buy cigarettes, and returned to the convenience store. She walked in just as I handed the clerk my credit card. She hardly noticed me; she was staring at the package of cigarettes. I guessed that she had once smoked, and was toying with the idea of taking it up again.

Once I paid the clerk, I lingered in front of the store and lit a cigarette, wanting to see her again. See how she appeared in the stark glare of the fluorescent light.

When she came out, she seemed lost in thought for a moment, but when she saw me she smiled suddenly, looking confident and glowing. When she smiles, she is pretty. When she isn't smiling, she is only attractive. Her face is narrow, her mouth too wide. Of average height, maybe a little below, her posture is erect. Yet she walks in a halting way, as if she could suddenly turn either to the right or the left. Her eyes are her best feature, a deep brown, focused at one moment, dissociated at the next.

She's younger than her husband, but not by much, maybe four or five years. Originally from New York, from what I've heard—that's where they met, before moving to Harrington.

Before I got into my car, I impulsively called out to her, asked if she was Dr. Forester's wife. I wanted to see her response. She nodded tentatively, avoiding my gaze; at that moment, she became impenetrable. I suppose I shouldn't have followed my impulse. But I've been doing so for so long, ever since my parents died. It is how I survive.

Eleven

Stephen, early July

Morning light streams into Stephen's office, illuminating the top of his desk and the sheet just printed from his laptop with the names of patients he'll see today. Foggy from a night of uneven sleep, he slowly picks up the list, and notices Eva Hathaway's name first. He winces, disconcerted but not certain why. It isn't that her symptoms and personality diagnosis are very different or more complex than most other patients. It's emotional on his part. And though he's only seen her twice, he doesn't like how he's thinking about Mrs. Hathaway. He believes something is inherently wrong.

Now that she's decided to come back to him, he thinks he should meet with Philip Barone about the case, but he doesn't have anything tangible to report at this point in the therapy. But then again, Philip has never been one to rely on what is manifestly evident.

When Stephen opens his office door, Mrs. Hathaway is in the waiting room, twenty minutes early. She appears taken aback by his sudden presence. Before he has a chance to tell her she's early and he'll see her at the appointed time, she collects her pocketbook and strides into his office. And he's more annoyed with himself than with her. For some reason he's not able to set boundaries.

She avoids his gaze and sits down, crosses her legs. Her expression is earnest and her eyes are pained, a murky blue today, more like the Mississippi than the Adriatic.

"I know you believe I was angry at our last meeting," she says, her voice thoughtful, exacting. She seems to be looking out beyond the window, maybe at the construction going on across the street, he thinks, following her gaze.

"You wanted me to talk about the bruise I got when I fell off the counter at the store where my father worked. Because, I suppose, you believe my parents were negligent . . . Oh, yes, I may have been angry with you for a day or two, but that isn't the reason I've stayed away for three weeks. The truth is I'm uncertain whether or not I should tell you more of my story."

"Don't feel you must say anything. If you don't wish to see me anymore, if you think I'm not helping you, I can refer you to another psychiatrist. You must think of yourself, not me, to get to the bottom of what's disturbing you, Mrs. Hathaway . . . Eva."

He's said the same thing many times to other patients, but without the same sense of urgency and restlessness.

Still she looks past him, doesn't respond to his words, and says quietly, "I need to tell you about Happenings, and so I've come back. Regarding the bruise— I didn't know about the bruise until I was older, eleven, I believe. My father's sister, my aunt Lora, told me I'd fallen off the counter the day my father received the letter. I don't remember falling or hitting my head. But I do remember Happenings, and my father playing jazz piano there when I was very young, after he received the letter."

"If you need to speak about Happenings, please do so," Stephen says impassively. She is making a concerted effort to be straightforward with him today, though he's uncertain whether or not he will be able to help her therapeutically. Clearly something is missing in this therapy, he thinks, again blaming himself.

"Happenings was always smoke-filled and dark, and when Father played, the melody seemed to echo in an odd way, almost disharmoniously. The acoustics were good, but not good enough to allow for his talent to be fully appreciated. He produced an incredible sound, unlike anything I've ever heard, even after all these years."

"Did you hear him play somewhere with better acoustics?"

"Yes. I knew how good he was because I was with him when he practiced at the community center where he'd worked as a janitor years before. The acoustics there were exceptional. His former boss allowed him to use the piano to rehearse. My mother and I would go with him, and he'd practice for hours. She'd make a picnic. We'd sit on a blanket on the floor of the auditorium, eating sandwiches, and she'd peel an apple. I would fall asleep on her knee while Father played."

"This was after he began to work at Happenings?"

"Yes, for a few years, until he was able to buy a piano of his own. That was the happiest time of my life—when we'd have a picnic on the floor of the auditorium while my father practiced the piano."

Stephen thinks she doesn't look very happy recollecting this time, but pensive, intense, as if she is about to strike her fist against the arm of the chair.

He nods, encouraging her to say more.

"But on the nights we went to Happenings, I was mostly sad, except when I sat in the coat check room with Claudia, the young woman who worked there. And I also recall those misty evenings when I'd walk with my parents from the parking lot into the nightclub; I smelled the ocean but could not see it.

"Though for the most part, my memories of Happenings are obscure. At times I'd become very tired, and my mother would send me to the room in the back to lie down on the sofa. It was a beige color, lumpy, too soft. The room was dark, and I felt closed in, as if I were in a closet. There was no window, and I was frightened. But I was so tired I couldn't get up. Every once in a while someone would come in, and I'd call out for my mother."

"They left you alone?"

"I don't remember. You see, Doctor, Happenings interfered with our happiness. We were all happy until a certain point, even my mother, who was edgy most of the time, and often defensive."

"Did your father still work in Rocco's store when he played at Happenings?"

"He did for a while, until he was able to support us by playing the piano. He never made a lot of money. My mother became his business manager. She found other places for him to work, other clubs. And when she secured such opportunities for him, he was able to leave his job at Rocco's store."

"Why were you so unhappy at the nightclub? You were with your parents."

She now looks directly at him, waiting a few minutes before answering. "Yes, but my father was often sad when he was there—I'd feel his melancholy. He began to drink when he worked at Happenings, and there is more, as you have surmised."

She hesitates, not certain whether or not to say more. He can see her indecision. Restlessly she taps her foot on the rug, and then swivels slowly from side to side in the chair, as if pondering what to say next.

"Aunt Lora's husband, Mario, went to Happenings," she says, her voice uneasy.

"You weren't partial to her husband?"

"I didn't like him, because she seemed different from the Aunt Lora I knew when she was with him. Though I believe she loved him. She was less vibrant, less interested in things when they were together. It was as if she were chained to him in some way. At the same time, I realized this was her choice. She could have walked away from him. Women did leave their husbands—it didn't commonly happen, but it wasn't unusual, especially if there were no children involved. And she had a job; she worked at Woolworth's, not full time, but in the mornings from nine to noon, or sometimes in the early afternoon."

"So this aunt you adored, you saw her both as an independent woman, and a dependent woman at the same time—emotionally dependent, perhaps?"

"Yes, yes," Eva promptly says. But Stephen believes her mind is elsewhere.

When Eva leaves his office, Stephen begins to pace. Then he stops to look out the window, watches her crossing the parking lot. She is trying to provoke him in some way, he believes. And she's hiding something important. Abruptly his thoughts shift to Brea. Although she's denied it, he wonders if she's hiding something as well.

Eva's Journal

I was riding the train, returning home from school when I met my first husband. At Aunt Lora's insistence I attended a Catholic college for women. It was the late 1960s, an electric time. Although there were anti-war protests going on at many colleges, our campus was quiet and sedate.

We were taught by lay professors as well as by nuns. The nuns wore skirts that fell just below their knees and white head caps with short veils. The lay professors, both men and women, were quiet and unobtrusive. This college environment was calming, allaying my impulsive nature during classes, but once I took the train home, I'd again feel anxious and restless. My sixteenth and seventeenth years had been traumatic ones, and each day as I rode the train home from the college, thoughts of what had happened during that time would haunt me. That was, until I met my first husband, Richard Stein.

He sat across from me, and when the train suddenly stopped in the middle of the tunnel, we made eye contact. I was attracted to him; I felt his intensity. His eyes were small but deep, incisive, his lashes long, and his brows dark and wispy. His features were even, and he had a small mole on his left cheek. I smiled, and he got up, came across the aisle and sat next to me, his steady expression never changing.

"How long do you think we'll be stuck here?" he asked, his voice grainy.

I shrugged. It was a cold day in late January, the beginning of the new term. "For a while," I answered, and looked directly into his eyes, noting a trace of fear.

"Where are you from?" he asked.

"I get off at the next stop."

"Your name?"

"Eva Morelli."

"Richard Stein," he said, looking away from me, his hands on his thighs, as if he might get up and return to his seat. I didn't want him to leave. His dark eyes revealed a natural intelligence I'd sensed from across the aisle.

"Are you from Boston?" I asked, trying to detain him.

"No," he said. "I go to school in Boston."

"School?"

"Law."

"But you're traveling in the opposite direction."

"I have an apartment three stops away."

"So you get off two stops after mine."

"I guess I do."

"Get off with me," I said impulsively, daringly.

His gaze was even but I knew he was taken aback by my directness and was making an effort not to show he'd been jarred by it. He turned away, as if considering whether or not to agree, and at that moment the train began moving.

"You don't have much time to decide," I said.

His look was quizzical, as if he was uncertain whether I was a little crazy, or simply earnest and honest.

Then just as the train came to another abrupt stop, he nodded and said, "Okay."

I had been through so much, and wasn't apprehensive. When you've experienced what I have, you lose your fear, perhaps to the extreme.

As we sat facing one another in the coffee shop close to the station, I put my hand over his. He looked both surprised and touched. Although he was in his mid-twenties, there were lines about his eyes, as if he worried too much, and this made him look older. I intuitively knew he had more character than I would ever have. And I believe that was what caused me to love him immediately and intensely.

"You're lonely," he said, squinting.

"I have reason to be," I answered, looking away. "And you?"

His voice was warm and terse at the same time. "I suppose I am, whenever I'm free—those moments when no one else is around—I do feel lonely. But I'm so busy that it doesn't happen very often, and so I forget those times; they don't stay with me," he said carefully.

"Do you live alone?" I asked.

He nodded. "Do you live with your parents?"

"My parents are dead. They passed away a few years ago. I live with my aunt."

"Is she good to you?"

"Yes, but she was better before my parents died. Now she's nervous with me, anxious. She never had any children, and suddenly she has a grown-up one. It's difficult for her. But she tries."

When we left the coffee shop, we ambled back to the train station holding hands. As the train roared into the station, he held me close and kissed me.

I waved as he boarded, losing sight of him once he found a seat. Although he'd taken my number, I believed I'd never hear from him again. He may not have liked my forwardness. But he did call the next night, and we went on our first date that weekend.

We met at the same coffee shop. It was a biting cold day, and when he walked through the door I didn't recognize him at first. He'd wrapped a red and blue scarf round his neck and most of his face. He came over, but didn't sit on the counter stool next to me. "I have my car today," he said.

When I stood up, I realized that in my boots I was an inch taller than Richard. Intuitively I slouched. He put his arm around me and said, "Stand tall, Eva."

It took a while for the heat in his car to come on. But once it did, I took off my hat, felt my hair fall past my shoulders. He smiled. And I felt gratified, believing he was now at ease.

We went to a movie—I can't remember the name of it. But I felt melancholic when it was over. It was about a broken relationship, involving two young people living in Eastern Europe.

Though it was late in the day when we left the cinema, the wind had died down and it was not as cold as before. And I had an idea, an impulse. I reached for

his hand. "Richard," I said, "I want to show you something." He looked surprised, but nodded his head.

When we got to his car, I told him where to drive. At
first he seemed impatient with my directions, but soon
he appeared interested. I believed I'd piqued his
curiosity. After thirty minutes or so, I told him to pull
over to the side of the road.

"What? Why? This is a cemetery," he said defiantly.

"Exactly," I said.

And we sat in silence, the motor still running. I
waited until it dawned on him why we were there. After
a few minutes, he looked over at me and said quietly,
"Your parents."

Their tombstone was close to the gate, just across
the street from where we left the car. We held hands as
we stood on the sidewalk, waiting for cars to pass.
Once the road was clear, we crossed quickly. For different reasons, we both wanted to get it over with.

"Ledo and Rose Morelli," he read aloud as we stood
before their tombstone. When I went over and touched
the top of it, I felt the cold marble through my glove. The
wind began to pick up again. I shivered and felt tears
coming to my eyes. It frightened me that I'd brought him
there. Then he came over to me, took my hand, and we
hurried back to the car.

As we drove toward his apartment in the suburbs,
we made small talk. He said it was good to have a day
off from his studies. And I told him I didn't know yet
what I wanted to do with my life. I felt uncertain and
apprehensive and believe he was as well.

Soon we passed a few large Victorian homes with
spacious front porches, then rows of tall naked trees.
Just as a light snow began to fall, he pulled into the

driveway of a white two-story colonial house. His apartment was on the first floor.

There was a fireplace in his bedroom. He crouched before the screen, pushed it aside, tucked newspapers under the logs, and then struck a match.

I sat at the edge of his bed, my boots off, my stockings damp from the cold. He came over and knelt down, gently placing his hands over my thighs. My legs tensed. And he smiled.

"I think I understand you, Eva," he said, his voice pensive. "You are mostly sad, very sad and lonely. But there is another side of you that is lively, that longs for an exuberant life."

We lay down next to one another on the bed, fully dressed, holding hands. The only sound came from the crackling fire. After a while one of us began to laugh—I don't recall if it was me or Richard. And then the other joined in. Soon we embraced, caressing one another, still laughing.

The following year, my senior year of college, we were living together. His parents did not approve of me. They found me to be dreamy and aloof, thought I should have a career in mind. Richard understood. He knew I needed time to heal, to grow. At twenty-one, he often said, you're both younger and older than most people your age.

Invariably he was busy, in his last year of law school, on the law review, and this preoccupied him. The following year, during his clerkship for a prominent judge, I didn't see him enough, and thought about leaving him. But I didn't because when we were together, it was always as intense and emotional as it had been from the start of our relationship.

The next year we were married by a justice of the peace. I never told Richard the complete story of my parents' death, and what happened to me soon afterward; my error of omission led to our eventual divorce. For inadvertently he discovered the truth. Someone from my hometown had come to work in his office, and told him the story. I hadn't been fully honest with him—I couldn't be, as I loved him too much. And when Richard told me what he'd heard, I revealed even more: what had happened to me the year following their deaths. It was the first time I had disclosed all there was to know about me.

I was relieved he knew the truth, and told him so. Yet from that day onward, he never quite trusted me. And when there's a loss of trust, there's also a loss of passion. There were no children, and so it was easier to part. We had lived together for five years, and had been married for nearly three of them.

I hear from him occasionally. He's been married for twenty-five years to the same woman. Bill and I will have a drink with him and his wife whenever they come to Boston. They have two sons, and I know all about them, as he knows about our children, Jesse and Amber. During our meetings, Richard will be open and warm. Yet even though so much time has passed, I know he's never really forgiven me—it's as if I deprived him of something he wanted terribly.

Twelve

Brea, early July

Brea paces in her study with the script in her hand. When she hears a cough, she looks over at the doorway where Stephen stands, shaking his head. "Let it go for a moment, Brea, let it go—it's close to midnight," he says sharply.

She's stunned by his comment, thinks of rehearsing the scene tomorrow with Sam, and is about to argue with him when she sees the fatigue in his eyes. Instead she shrugs, stretches out her arms and goes over to him. She throws her arms around his neck and lightly kisses his lips, feeling the pressure of his chest against hers. Smiling, she recalls how kind he was when she was under the weather last week. He'd put pillows under her feet, had made her a cup of black tea. And she feels a sharp yearning within—it's been too long, she thinks.

"Stephen, you look tired. You must have had an exhausting day. You need rest," she says, pressing her finger to his lips.

Soon she feels his hand grasping hers, his eyes now alert. "I'm not that tired," he says; she hears longing in his voice.

"Fuck Mrs. Alving!" she cries out, flinging the script across the room.

Thirteen

Stephen, early July

"The independent/dependent nature of your Aunt Lora you described during our last session—do you think this had anything to do with why she refused to come to the nightclub?"

"Oh, yes, it had everything to do with why she wouldn't go to Happenings," Eva half smiles and says, "You're beginning to understand."

"Beginning to understand?" Stephen asks, his voice mellow, but he feels a sense of apprehension, and is convinced there is something unsettling occurring in this therapy. He studies her. Is she or isn't she hiding something? he wonders.

"Father played on the stage, in a corner close to the bar. The nightclub wasn't very large, and so his music filled the room. People left dollar bills in a glass bowl on top of the piano. There was one man who came every so often. No one knew his name, and my father called him Mr. Green because he always left a very generous tip. My mother usually sat at the table closest to the piano, drinking a club soda, and Mr. Green would sit with her and talk. My parents looked forward to seeing Mr. Green, not only because of the tips he left. He was quite attractive in a way that was pleasing to both men and women, according to Mother. I remember at times she was more nervous at Happenings, her face too flushed, even more than when she was at home."

"Do you think she may have been less nervous when she spoke with the generous Mr. Green?"

"I imagine that she was. One night, according to Mother, Mr. Green came in, and before he went to speak with her, he went over and talked to Uncle Mario. Mother said Mr. Green was always quiet and well mannered. But that night, after five minutes or so, Mr. Green and Mario began to argue. Or rather, it was Uncle Mario who yelled at Mr. Green, while Mr. Green listened, and didn't respond.

"Mother abruptly left Happenings, and drove me home before Father finished for the evening—something she'd never done before. All I remember about that night is sitting next to her in the car as she made her way across a heavy steel bridge, her small hands clutching the steering wheel. Splashing rain covered the windshield, the wipers moving frantically. She stared straight ahead, her body erect as if she were frightened. A few days later, Uncle Mario died. He had a stroke. And I refused to go back to Happenings because I believed in a way my uncle died there—I associated it with his death—a deathly place."

"It must have been very traumatic," Stephen says.

"At the time, yes. After that I could not remember what Mr. Green looked like, or if I'd ever seen him at Happenings. In my mind, he never existed. Over the next few years from time to time I'd try to envision Mr. Green—force myself to recall him, but I couldn't. It's unfathomable, Doctor Forester. Yet it was even more traumatic later. Much, much more than you realize," she says, her large eyes filling with tears.

Stephen studies her. The harder I listen, the less I hear, he thinks.

Eva's Journal

Following her husband's death Aunt Lora was quite distraught. But I realized it only gradually. For at first she appeared much the same—more weary and preoccupied than she'd been, but not significantly so. She continued to visit us after she finished work, ending her visit at five o'clock as she had in the past, as if she were going home to make dinner for her husband. She never mentioned Mario, but that wasn't unusual because she never talked much about him when he was alive. So in a sense, at first, it wasn't as if anything significant had happened.

But about a year or so later, she unexpectedly quit her job at Woolworth's. Now she stayed home all day. When I saw how forlorn she'd become, I wondered if I'd misjudged her husband, their marriage. I'd visit her after school every day, try to cheer her up. I was fourteen at the time.

One wintry afternoon in early March, as I approached her house I noticed a car in front of her driveway. I was too far away to see the make or model, and then the car suddenly sped away.

When Aunt Lora came to the door, she was in her robe. Her eyes were red, as if she'd been crying. "Come in, Eva," she said, half-heartedly. And for the first time I thought she didn't want me there. Should I leave? I wondered. I stood in the doorway, not knowing what to do. "Come in, Eva," she said and pressed her hand to her forehead as if she had a headache.

"You are tired, Aunt Lora. Are you sure you want company today?" I asked, looking directly at her.

"Yes, Eva," she said firmly, her eyes avoiding mine. She motioned for me to come in, and we both went into her living room and sat opposite one another.

She appeared older that day, worried. I hadn't seen her languid, dreamy side for so long. Most of all I missed her humor. My parents were too serious, and now very unhappy.

For after Uncle Mario's death, my father drank even more. And when he'd been drinking too much, he'd push Mother and sometimes strike her. But he never touched me. One night their arguing woke me. I ran downstairs to the kitchen, saw my mother grab a bottle of whiskey from his hand. Then he reached out and slapped her hard across the face. She staggered back and fell against the counter, hitting her head. I gasped and ran to her, held her in my arms. Her body felt sturdy and tight. "Stay away from her!" I screamed, tears running down my face. Father turned away and left. Soon I heard him stumbling up the stairs.

I looked down at Mother. "He's tired, Eva," she whispered, her eyes half-open.

Increasingly frustrated by my mother's acceptance of my father's drinking, I spent more and more time with Aunt Lora.

And so on that early March day I felt especially unsettled by Aunt Lora's solemn expression, the trouble in her hazel eyes.

"Would you like me to make tea?" I asked. When I got up from the chair, she held out her hand to stop me.

"No, Eva, not today."

"I saw a car drive away," I said.

"Come here, Eva," she said, patting the sofa cushion, "come sit next to me."

I went to her and leaned my head against her comforting arm. "What's wrong?" I asked, impulsively. "Who was the person who drove off? Someone you know?" I moved away from her and sat up straight, clenching my fists, fearful I would lose someone so dear to me.

She seemed unconcerned by my insistence. "Eva, I have a story to tell you, so listen carefully, and promise to tell no one. It can be a secret between us." She began to sound more like her old self. Smiling, she rested her head back against the cushion, her expression hopeful and distinguished.

"What is it, Aunt Lora?" I got up from the sofa and knelt before her. "What are you hiding from me?"

"I don't hide things, Eva—you should know that."

"But you said, it was a secret," I cried out.

She looked weary, and I wondered if she regretted her words. But soon she recovered, and looked composed. "You're such a funny girl, Eva. Well, I don't know if I should call you a girl—you're fourteen, or is it fifteen now?" She smiled, her voice teasing.

She patted the sofa with her hand again, inviting me to sit next to her. "You are a bit intimidating, kneeling before me in that way." She laughed, pressed her fingers to her lips, her shoulders swaying as if the joke were on her, not on me.

I was delighted by the change in her, and sat next to her. Her eyes shone, almost a golden color as she rubbed her hand over mine. "You're beautiful. Never think otherwise. You're beautiful when you're relaxed and confident. When you become fearful and worried, it takes away from your beauty, more so than other beautiful women. You must remember this."

"Is this the secret you wanted to tell me?"

"No, Eva darling, I wish it was that simple. It's very complicated and you may not understand it fully now, but someday you will."

"Why me?" I asked suddenly.

"For now you're the only one I can tell. And you must not breathe a word to anyone. Maybe someday you will . . . when the time seems right . . . but I imagine that won't be for a long time. You must promise."

"I promise," I said, but was unsure, not ready for the responsibility. Yet I could not disappoint her. She was everything to me.

I braced myself and gazed into in her hazel eyes, soft and concerned. She looked away, as if to focus on a distant memory.

"You see, Eva dear, I'm in love."

"I know you loved Uncle Mario very much." I answered, bowing my head in deference to their marriage, despite my skepticism about it.

"Yes, that's true, and I miss him terribly. But you see, Eva, I'm in love with someone else right now. And it bothers me, but it's true. I cannot deny it or fight it anymore."

"Are you planning to marry him? Is that your secret?"

"No, Eva, I don't know if I'll marry again, or maybe someday we will be married, but right now I'm going to live with him."

"No," I said and drew away. "I won't see you anymore, and how is that a secret? Everyone will know you've left your home."

"First of all, you will see me. I'll keep my home. I'll live here on weekends, and live with him during the week for one or two days, sometimes three. So you and I will be able to meet and talk as we do now. That won't be bad, will it?" she asked, and smiled at me in her caring and vivacious way.

"How will my parents not know about this ?" I asked in disbelief. My head was swimming.

"This is where you can help. I want you still to come every day after school, as if I were here. Tell your mother you're going to Aunt Lora's home. That won't be a lie, as you will be coming here. I'll give you a key."

"What if someone calls, wants to reach you?"

"I want you to answer the phone for me—you can say Aunt Lora is busy right now; she'll call you soon."

"How will I reach you?"

"I'll call you every evening at five to find out if anyone has tried to get in touch with me. Are you willing to help, Eva?" she asked earnestly, her eyes fixed on mine.

I looked at her, saw her excitement and her desperation. I was overwhelmed and frightened, yet dared not refuse.

"Yes, I will help you!" I cried out and threw my arms round her. As she held me close, tears streamed down my face. For my sense of the truth was slipping away.

Fourteen

Brea, early July

On break from rehearsal, Brea stands on the sidewalk in front of the lingerie store in the town center, takes the cigarette from her mouth, and holds it at a distance, studying it. A damnable habit, she thinks. What an example she is to Ned, who'd been shocked when he saw her smoking. His mouth had dropped open, and he'd grown pale as she came from her study with the cigarette between her fingers. But, oh, how difficult it is to be honest with your child and at the same time be thoroughly human. When she hugged him, he was warm and wiry; yet soon she felt him withdraw from her arms.

She loves him intensely, oh so intensely. It was only a cigarette, but you would have thought he'd caught her stealing. She was chagrinned, and the memory brings back the unease she felt at the time. She must stop smoking immediately, or at least when the play is over in mid-August. But smoking may affect the quality of her voice.

She feels a drop of rain on her shoulder, stamps out the cigarette, and goes inside the lingerie shop, regretting she's given Ned permission to ride his bicycle along the wharf. She hopes he'll be as careful as he always is. She remembers how adventurous she was at twelve—taking the subway into Times Square with her friends, not telling her mother. Will Ned become as precocious as she was if they move back to New York?

Today she didn't refuse Ned when he asked because he's been so good-natured this summer. He hasn't complained that she often refuses to take him to the ocean. The rainy weather this past week has been her excuse, but mostly it is because she has been preoccupied with the Mrs. Alving role, despite that momentary sense of comprehension she experienced a few weeks ago when she saw the woman outside the convenience store who asked if she were Dr. Forester's wife. And so Brea has been diligently rehearsing her lines again and again in hope of improving her understanding of Mrs. Alving.

There is no other customer in the store; the two saleswomen are deep in conversation. Brea easily finds the sale table. She picks up a black negligee. While holding it up, she thinks about the rehearsal this morning.

To her surprise, Sam, who usually is very much a hands-on director, is hands-off in this production. He stays in the background as much as he can, not commenting very much, just nodding as if things are fine. But they aren't! She isn't satisfied with her acting and despite her past silent criticisms of Sam as a director, his literal approach, his constant interruptions that effect her concentration, she wishes he'd now employ his former methods. Maybe that would help. No, she doesn't like that he is less involved as a director this time, and more involved as an actor, she thinks. She puts down the black negligee, decides it's not for her.

Can Sam be pleased with how the rehearsals are progressing? How can he be, when she is so miserable?

She's becoming more and more drawn to him, she realizes. But she's known him for ten years—why now?

As she walks out of the lingerie shop without having purchased anything, she pulls out another cigarette from her handbag and lights it.

Hastily she glances at her watch. It is time to head back to the theater. The clouds are now thick and dark. It might rain some more, she thinks, her thoughts scattering as she feels a sudden hard tap on her shoulder. Intuitively, she knows it is Sam.

"Brea," he says.

"Hi, Sam." She drops the cigarette, and hastily snuffs it out with her sandal. As they walk towards the theater, the sun unexpectedly peeks out from behind the clouds, and she notices wrinkles around his eyes, a few strands of gray in his hair. It occurs to her that she's only one year younger than Sam.

"Sam," she says, looking up at him. "I can't believe we've been working together for ten years—it's gone by in a flash."

"Yes, Brea, ten years, and while I've aged, you still look the same."

"Oh, Sam, you are too kind, and probably not as cynical as I once thought," she says, hoping he takes note of her mild sarcasm. Yet she longs to throw her arms around him, press her face into his chest.

"You think I haven't noticed how good you look?"

"Why are you saying this now?" she asks, her heart beating quickly; she stops walking just as the sun disappears again and it begins to rain.

"You think I haven't been interested?"

She feels the intensity of his voice, and as the rain pelts her back, she closely studies his brown-gray eyes.

Her throat tightens. "I don't really know," she says, hearing an edge in her voice.

Eva's Journal

I blindly followed Aunt Lora's instructions, never inquiring about her lover, his name or where he lived. Every day after school I went to her home. When she wasn't there, I'd leave the back door open for a few hours while I did my homework. And although I didn't yet have my license, I'd back her car out of the garage and leave it in the driveway.

If the phone rang I'd answer and say that Aunt Lora had gone to the grocery store. Stealthily I'd wait for five o'clock and Aunt Lora's call. Once she phoned I'd give her the name and number of anyone who'd called.

One afternoon the neighbor next door phoned. When I told her Aunt Lora was at the grocery store, she said she'd called because she'd noticed her car in the driveway. Thinking fast, I told her I'd meant to say that Aunt Lora had walked to the corner store, not the grocery store. When she didn't respond immediately, my heart began to pound. But soon she told me she was taking up a collection of clothes for the poor, and wanted to know if Aunt Lora had something to donate. Tell her to call me, she said.

After I hung up the phone, I went to the sink and turned on the faucet, splashing water on my face to calm myself.

When I told Aunt Lora about the call, she was concerned at first, but after she thought about it for a few minutes she said her neighbor wasn't one to bother with other people's business. Nonetheless, when Aunt Lora returned home two days later, she gathered her old clothes together, delivered them to her neighbor, and stayed to have coffee with her.

Because my parents were unaware of what was going on around them, they were heedless of how Aunt Lora's life had changed. Mother now spent nearly all of her time setting up playing engagements for my father. During this time they often traveled to places outside the community, to different parts of the state, as well as to clubs in New York. For by then, my father was a well-respected jazz pianist.

They were often away on weekends, and I would stay with Aunt Lora until they returned. During the week, Father played at Happenings and since they got home so late every night, they slept in, and when I returned home from school, and Aunt Lora's house, they would be eating and getting ready to leave for the show. I'd walk into the kitchen and hear them discuss the music he would play that evening, or some gossip about the owner of Happenings. Father would sit at the table with a glass of scotch in hand while my mother served him dinner.

One Monday evening I came in as Mother was opening the oven door. When she heard me, she looked up, her face flushed from the heat. She asked if I'd seen Aunt Lora that day. When I told her I was at her home that afternoon, she stared at me and said, "Eva, are you telling the truth?" Her tone was sharp.

I nodded, but felt disconcerted.

"I've been calling her all day, and she hasn't answered," she said.

I swallowed because I knew she hadn't phoned during the two-hour time I'd been there. "She wasn't feeling very well, and has been resting all day. She might have been sleeping when you called," I answered forthrightly; my loyalty to my aunt superseded my fear of being caught in a lie. Mother didn't say anything; she just continued to stare at me. Then Father walked in and after lightly kissing my forehead, he turned to her and said he was in the mood to play some Johnny Mercer that night. I smelled alcohol on his breath and was pained, thinking of the times I'd seen him strike her.

Appearing uneasy, my mother studied me. When my father drew her attention away by mentioning particular songs, I slipped out of the kitchen and stayed in my room until they left.

The next day Aunt Lora called at five o'clock, and I told her what had happened. Promptly she phoned my mother to explain she'd been in bed with the flu.

Covering for Aunt Lora became the focal point of my life. I was completely preoccupied with helping her, keeping her secret with an intensity I cannot describe. I believed I needed to protect her, not only because she was good to me, but because I wanted her to be happy.

During that time I often ruminated over Aunt Lora's situation instead of concentrating on my homework, and so my grades began to suffer. I had one friend, but it wasn't a very close friendship, more of a convenient one, and I didn't date at all. I was interested in boys, but boys my age seemed immature.

One afternoon, heading over to Aunt Lora's, I passed the movie theater. Outside the ticket booth, standing in line, I saw a group of girls and boys from my class. Some were chattering excitedly, others laughing; they did not notice me. And I was startled—my heart began to race, tears came to my eyes. I longed to be with them. As I walked on, it struck me that I was imprisoned in Aunt Lora's world.

Soon I came up with an idea. It pleased me so much I sat up all night thinking about it. I was excited, as I believed it would be adventurous to carry off a plan of my own. Once I went through with it, the burden Aunt Lora had placed on me would be lifted. I'd be free to live as I wished.

Fifteen

He gazes over at Brea sleeping next to him. The blinds are half-drawn; a strip of light crosses her forehead, which is smooth and high, exuding quiet intelligence. Her closed eyelids appear uneasy. More determined than most, he thinks—yet when least expected she can be quite yielding. This causes him unease.

When they'd been together for six months or so— *The Importance of Being Earnest* having just closed— she auditioned for a part in a play by a new and upcoming playwright, on Broadway this time. It was a small part, so small that she was afraid it would be written out of the production. She practiced the two lines over and over in front of the mirror on the bedroom door. They'd chosen to live in his apartment on the East Side; it was close to the hospital and not far from the off-Broadway theater where she usually worked.

Every evening she tried a new approach, and was elated with some of her attempts, discouraged by others. Stephen supported her, always thought the latest one was by far the best. Purposely he'd speak in an understated way, and she'd look at him pensively and think it over before coming to a decision. If he'd been more exuberant or indifferent, she might not have believed him, he now thinks. But she had found his reactions sincere, and she began to trust him more and more.

Although she did not get the part in the play, she didn't resent the actress who did; in any event, by the time the play opened the role was written out of the script.

He recalls her standing before the mirror in her silk underclothes, the pink chemise and matching loose silk shorts fringed in lace caressing her thighs. Every night she worked so diligently, so assiduously, thinking up different possible interpretations while he sat on the bed nodding approval. He liked watching the change in her expression; she'd become flustered, or radiant, or deeply disappointed. Even more than her dramatic efforts, he relished her personal reactions. This didn't seem to bother her—she had so much good will.

But once she reproached him. "Oh, you don't care, Stephen. You like me. You don't care what I do. It doesn't matter to you." He felt her tension at that moment.

With one hand she ruffled her hair and came over to him, kissing him hard on the mouth. Then she drew away, threw back her head, broadly smiling. Lightly, he tickled her neck. She grasped his arm, and they laughed, and made love in the same fervent mood. Yet an hour or two later, he was filled with uncertainty again.

Now he gets out of bed, goes over to the window and looks down at the front lawn; the roses are withered and drooping, no longer in bloom. Then he turns and watches Brea stirring in her sleep. Again he thinks how when least expected, she can be so yielding.

Later, having breakfast out on the deck, sitting across from her, he sees she's wearing a light gray halter dress he doesn't recognize. As she gets up to go into the kitchen to get another spoon, he notices how much of her back and waistline are exposed and his pulse quickens.

When she returns, he uneasily catches her gaze and says, "I've been thinking about my presentation. It's only about six weeks away."

"Yes, Stephen—we'll be done with *Ghosts* by then. It's a short run, no more than three weeks. And after all the effort we're putting into the rehearsals." She seems less enthusiastic than usual. But he knows: first, excitement over a new role, then her preparations; invariably she's exacting in her approach. A week before the performance doubts creep in, a certain lack of enthusiasm. By opening night, she'll be as ready and as probing as always.

"But all the effort is worth it, Brea."

She studies him for a moment; her eyes sharp. "I suppose," she says, caustically, briskly buttering her toast.

Working against him and not with him, he thinks. Perhaps it's because she wants to leave Harrington sooner than he is able to. He would like to talk about his presentation, but she's too moody about the play. He's always gone along with her moods, never fought them with his own agenda. Her moodiness usually excites him, but today he's discouraged by it.

He thinks about his father, regretting that he never met Brea. He would have thought her attractive, but perhaps found her too unrestrained. Ironic, he thinks. His father's intent was to free people through his work.

"The art and science of listening—that's what you'll be talking about in Florence, isn't it?" Brea asks, her voice matter-of-fact as she pours more coffee into each cup.

Stephen feels encouraged by her question. "Yes, of course. It's funny, when I started writing, I didn't intend to go in this direction, a discussion of listening—but I just naturally have. Maybe it's my way of taking the focus off me, the practitioner. I don't know." He falls silent as he thinks of Eva Hathaway. When it comes to her, his ability to listen has been compromised, and he isn't certain why.

"Brea, I've decided I will call Philip Barone to discuss a patient who's been on my mind lately."

"You think Philip can help?"

"Undoubtedly," he says, reaching out to grasp her hand, which feels hot and prickly.

Eva's Journal

Yesterday was the hottest day of summer yet. When I awoke, the heat was overpowering. Covers off, I lay still in bed, smothered by the warmth, leafy shadows crossing the blinds.

My appointment with Dr. Forester was not until noon, and I wasn't ruminating over what I'd say to him as I usually did before one of our sessions. Instead I was beginning to regret that I'd gone to him in the first place, the truth now seeming more elusive than ever.

As I drove to his office I decided I'd talk about my parents' deaths. Lately I've been having dreams of my mother when she was younger, her face flushed, her freckles startlingly visible, as if she were a ruddy porcelain doll. It was a sign, I thought, that I should tell him about what had happened to them. I was ready to reveal this very painful part of my life, and now trusted him enough to do so.

But from the beginning of our meeting it was clear he wanted to discuss my current marriage. Of course Dr. Forester wasn't obvious, as he's never been obvious with me. He wore an off-white linen suit and his demeanor was neither agitated nor calm. He was in that in-between state, preventing me from intuiting how he was feeling or what he was contemplating.

He began by referring to my water dream, which I hadn't spoken about since my first visit. I was disappointed, because I needed to speak about my parents' deaths. Discussing my water dream was less important, as it was fading away. I hadn't had it in weeks. But I soon realized he was focusing on my dream not to analyze it, but to encourage me to speak about my marriage. He didn't mention my fear of water, or ask for more details about the dream—if it were indeed still recurring. Instead he said that in my dream my husband was with me—we were a couple, a central part of the dream. As he spoke he looked over at his notes on his laptop. Although it was extremely hot, he hadn't put on the air conditioning. Instead he had opened all the windows. We were somewhat comfortable because of a cross breeze and one ceiling fan. He didn't seem to be too disturbed by the weather, but remained impassive, and when he spoke about my husband he did so in a gentle, nearly off-handed way.

I wanted to tell him that I'd intended to talk about my parents' deaths. But for some reason I didn't. His questions about my marriage to Bill distracted me from what I had hoped to reveal to him.

"Your husband was in your dream," he said, his forehead moist from the heat. He turned his head and glanced at the notes on his laptop a second time.

I nodded. "Of course my husband would be in my dream. There's no other man in my life." I spoke firmly, but smiled immediately—I didn't want him to think of me as overly solemn. And I hoped to lighten the communication between us. The heat was becoming more intense, no longer any trace of the cross breeze. So I resorted to levity—or maybe, on second thought, it was irony.

Nonetheless, he smiled back at me, and I felt we connected—he possessed a sense of humor, at least.

"So you've been married for some time?"

"Yes. It's my second marriage."

"Second? I didn't know."

"Yes. My first marriage was short-lived—so I didn't think it essential to tell you about it." I smiled again to let him know I wasn't sorry about my divorce. But this time he didn't return my smile. Instead, he became more serious. I didn't want him to pry any further. I still feel raw whenever I think of why Richard left me. "We keep in touch though. He has two sons with his second wife. We didn't have any children. I think of our brief marriage as that of two people living together, and then going their separate ways—no children, no ties, no harm done." Now I knew not to smile.

"Yet you decided to marry, you didn't choose to simply live together. You made a commitment, even though there were no children. A broken commitment is disappointing no matter who makes the break."

He was trying to provoke me to say more, but if I had, much more would have come out, and he would be the one shaken to the core, not me. I've gone through so much because of it, because of what happened. But I *couldn't reveal to him why Richard and I parted because there was a connection to him, his life.*

"Yes, it was disappointing," I said, directly. He looked at me for a moment or two, his expression bemused, as if he didn't quite believe me. I continued. "Yes, Doctor, I've had a disappointing life in some respects, but not in others. Bill, my second husband, is not a disappointment. In fact, he rescued me."

"Rescued you?"

"Yes, he rescued me from what I was," I said and smiled.

Dr. Forester didn't respond; he remained still in his chair, waiting for me to continue. I closed my eyes and took a deep breath. Despite the heat, despite my deception, I longed to be unwaveringly truthful.

"You see, Doctor, I am not an honest person—or maybe this isn't so, maybe I've learned to be secretive— I was taught to be this way. And my inability to be forthright is why my first marriage didn't last. To this day my first husband Richard cannot and will not forgive me for not telling him the whole story. My rationale is that there is no whole truth—that truth is relative. That my past shouldn't have been of any consequence to him, that I had indeed transcended it; there had been no need for me to tell all. I've learned since my divorce all those years ago that some truths are relative but others are irrefutable. I should have revealed everything to Richard."

"Do you feel he would have still committed to you, married you, if you had told him everything?"

"He said he would have."

"And I assume you told the whole truth to your second husband before you married him." He paused

before and after he said the word "whole." I believe it was his way of showing irony, or maybe it was sarcasm.

"Bill was different. He didn't believe in rehashing the past. Goodness knows, he had his own past to worry about. Bill wasn't as much of a purist as Richard was. And that relieved me."

"Your husband doesn't know everything there is to know about you?"

"I've been married to him for nearly thirty years— things do come out over time, and when they do, they're never as severe because I can make them seem less so, especially with someone like Bill who doesn't feel the need to know everything."

"So you believe Bill rescued you, simply by not needing to know the truth about your past?"

"No, it is much more complicated than that—he rescued me because he accepted me, my personality, who I had become. Personal facts have never interested Bill. He liked—likes—my personality, and I don't believe Richard ever did. Richard found me quirky. But Bill did love me, so he married me, or made a commitment to me, as you like to say."

Dr. Forester stood up and went over to the window, opened it wider. It occurred to me that he did it so that I would pause and think before I said anything else; he wanted me to reveal more. He sensed my hesitation. I think he knew that despite my attempt to appear spontaneous, I weighed every thought, every word before I spoke. Going over to the window was his signal that he knew what I was doing, yet I knew he could never possibly know why. He must have thought it was simply a defect in my personality—a personality disorder, I've heard it is called.

When he turned round, and came back to his chair, I said, "You don't believe me, do you, Doctor?"

"What is there not to believe? And didn't you say truth is relative?"

"Maybe I haven't been accurate, maybe not believing me is not the right thing to say—you think I am too guarded—that I'm not expressing myself fully to you."

"You are careful in your choice of words."

"Yes, I am careful with words."

"And, I assume, your emotions as well. You were the one who said I didn't believe you were being honest with me, not I. In fact, I think you're being as honest as you are able to be."

I nodded, and felt he had won that round. But this wasn't about winning or losing because we were both losers in this situation—he just hadn't realized yet how much he was involved.

"Bill has never really cared about the past," I said, wanting this discussion to get back to Bill, not Richard.

"Why?" he said, shrugging his shoulders as if it weren't that serious of a question.

"Because he knows the past can lead you astray. He looks at people, at life, as constantly changing. We are different people at various points in our lives. Because of our experiences, we can never be who we were, or who we want to be."

"And so you were rescued by his philosophy?"

"Yes, I was rescued by his philosophy because I no longer felt guilty for omitting or not omitting certain parts of my life to others. When I met Bill, I felt free for the first time in my life."

"Were you invigorated?"

"Yes, extremely so."

"Had you been feeling much guilt before you met him—is that why?"

"No more than most, I suppose, but he helped me realize I was carrying a lot of guilt."

"But you said when you met Bill and became familiar with his philosophy, you no longer felt guilty."

"Yes, I did say that. But my guilt was silent, I didn't think about it—it just stayed deep within me, paralyzing me. Once I met Bill, I was free, because he allowed me to release it."

"You were hiding your guilt?"

"Yes, I was."

"Has it returned?

I shrugged.

"Are you hiding from it now?"

I didn't answer, as he had frozen me. I reached for a tissue, and wiped away the tears in my eyes that hadn't yet fallen to my face. There is always a box of tissues on the table next to the swivel chair. I'd never taken one before. When I left his office a few minutes later, I knew something of significance had been accomplished in this session—for we had connected.

Sixteen

Brea, mid-July

On stage, Brea takes a deep breath to maintain her composure. It's warm under the lights; she must be flushed, she thinks, pressing her hand to her face.

They've rehearsed for two hours without a break but nothing is coming together. It's overly hot in the theater, and the lights shine down on all the cast members like rays from the sun. It crosses her mind as it has for the past two weeks that Sam may not be capable of acting and directing simultaneously. The cast has been reading through the same scene again and again.

Sam slides back and forth between roles: Pastor Manders and director. He is difficult to predict, Brea thinks—so calm and assured at one moment, and so dark and uneasy at the next. Which role does he prefer? she wonders as she watches him. He stands at the other end of the stage, instructing the woman who is playing the character of Regina to move her head to the left and hold her hands behind her back. He isn't as involved as usual. And this summer he's apparently not intrigued by the beautiful college junior who plays Regina, not in pursuit of her, so unlike him. For every summer Sam becomes involved with a female intern. Last year it was a student from NYU. She was tall and willowy, appropriately naïve as Sam usually prefers, and quite impressionable. Brea observed how she was transformed from a shy, slightly nervous girl to a confident and expressive woman, all under Sam's direction. At the end of the summer, Sam told her that she had to go on with her life and forget about him. Brea remembers the look on the young woman's face when she left the theater. Brea had watched from a distance, seen her puzzled expression.

Later when Brea asked Sam about it, he said, "She's grown from the experience, Brea. She'll be a fine actress someday—she has so much talent."

Brea responded, "Well, Sam, has it occurred to you that you might instead have discouraged her? Maybe now she'll marry, have children, stay at home, and think of the theater or life as an actress with a good degree of cynicism."

"If that is the case, Brea, she wasn't cut out to be an actress after all. Talent isn't the only thing involved; it's also a matter of temperament—sustaining yourself. That is what you're so good at." And she had shrugged, nodding her head slightly, and walked away.

Now as she looks at the young woman playing Regina, not only does she see a more sophisticated person than the student last year, but she realizes

Sam is not the same either; he is a disinterested Sam, not wanting to seduce or be seduced by this young woman.

Brea lowers her eyes to the script, quickly reviewing her lines. She already knows her part, but likes to look at the words to see if she's missed something, maybe find a different slant, a meaning she hasn't yet realized that will help her better understand the character of Mrs. Alving. But she notices nothing. She looks over at Sam, feeling frustrated. He's still the director, speaking privately with one actor then the next, explaining what he wants.

When Sam comes over to her, he takes her by the arm and walks with her to the far side of the stage.

"Brea," he begins, hesitating, "I'm more or less happy with your interpretation of this scene. But I need something more, and I'm not certain what it is. You're usually good at figuring these things out." His expression is quizzical. "You are good, Brea, you know that. I want you to be better in this part, a little better. Do yourself justice."

She smiles wearily at him, nodding, too depleted to counter him. It is hot and it has been a long afternoon.

"Let's have a drink after rehearsal is over," he says in a whisper. "We can finish this discussion."

"Okay, but it can't be for long," she answers, drawing in her breath.

Twenty minutes later the rehearsal ends, and Brea and Sam are the last to leave. Most of the lights have been switched off and it is very dark as they make their way across the stage, using the exit sign as their guide. There is a hush inside the theater that Brea has always found invigorating—it's like a sigh before a release of emotion—dramatic emotion, completely ensconcing yourself within a character. There is apprehension, a sense of the unknown, uncertainty whether your interpretation and performance will reach the height you want it to. To Brea the hush represents that quiet moment before you begin your performance.

When they walk outside they are startled by the strong sun, the hush evaporating in the reality of daylight.

Brea's feelings are mixed as they make their way to the Harrington Inn where there is a small bar and a certain amount of privacy. When they climb the few steps into the brick-and-ivy covered building, she is moved by the feel of Sam's hand on her back, near her waist, and thinks that maybe she should not have worn the gray halter dress today. Yet she savors his touch as they cross the lobby to the small cave-like bar tucked into a corner. There are wooden chairs and tables; the air is stirred by a ceiling fan. She chooses a table farthest from the entranceway, and Sam sits across from her.

After she orders a drink—a glass of white wine— and Sam, a local beer, they talk about the play. Brea notices how Sam switches from the role of director to actor, depending on whether he's talking about Mrs. Alving or Pastor Manders. He's a complete actor, Brea thinks—still surprised by her realization. His understanding of Pastor Manders is better than hers of Mrs. Alving, she concedes.

"I am looking for a new interpretation of Mrs. Alving," Brea says, stamping her fist lightly on the table. "And therein lies my hesitation, and you say you

117

want me to be better—I'm trying not only to be better, but to be different. Mrs. Alving, more often than not, has been regarded as somewhat weak, not a straightforward woman. But I see her as being strong and complex—yes, at times weak, but her weakness shows her humanity, not a lack of strength."

"I can't quite buy that, Brea. Either she's strong or she's weak; either she's complex or she's not. How could a woman who went back to her husband, a known womanizer—how could she agree to build an orphanage in his memory—how is she possibly a strong character? No, I say Mrs. Alving is weak, and she attempts to redeem herself at the end by helping her son Osvald when he's dying."

"Oh, Sam—she isn't suddenly strong, her strength has been there her all the time—it's latent, stored up, and because of the times she lives in she can't release it until her son is dying. She must first be a mother."

"Wasn't she a wife as well?"

"Well, she had intended to leave her husband, but Pastor Manders dissuaded her from doing so."

"You see, Brea, it is Pastor Manders who is the complex character—he held this woman's future in the palm of his hands, and because she was weak, she listened to him. She should have left her husband."

"But he told her not to—he is the conventional one behind the façade of good-spiritedness. And so she had to suffer her husband's infidelities."

"She had a son."

"And her husband had a daughter with their maid."

"What were her feelings for Pastor Manders, do you think?" he asks coyly.

118

"Feelings?" Brea asks sharply, reaching inside her pocketbook for a package of cigarettes. When she realizes she can't smoke there, she holds up the package, crushes it in one hand, and throws it on the table. "Feelings?" Her voice is more even now. She realizes she's no longer thinking only of Mrs. Alving, she's questioning herself. "She has no feelings for him; she detests him because he ruined her life."

"Isn't hate a feeling?"

"Of course it is," she says. "But it's not a feeling you want to remember, and so you begin to think less and less of the person, and therefore hate eventually leads to disinterest."

"But doesn't hate linger—does it so easily evaporate?"

"It depends on the type of hate—there's a seething, passionate hate, and there's a dull hate, one that goes away in time."

"And so what type of hate does Mrs. Alving feel toward Pastor Manders?"

"I'm not certain yet, I just don't know," she says, urgently pressing her hand over his.

Eva's Journal

Late yesterday afternoon while Bill and I were sitting at a table in the bar at the Harrington Inn, Dr. Forester's wife, the actress, walked in with her director. They brushed past our table without looking at us.

Bill had had a meeting with his clients in one of the conference rooms, and so we'd agreed to meet at the bar to have a drink before dinner. Though I wasn't certain if she'd recognize me, I didn't want to take a chance, so I kept my back to her. I heard them walk over to a table in the far corner of the room, but it's a small room; the bar's to the left of the entranceway. I thought Bill might recognize Sam from the party where we met two years ago, so I pointed to the television behind the bar to distract him, and a news item that crossed the flat screen caught his attention.

Sam either didn't remember Bill, or didn't notice him, so that was good. I felt uneasy, regretted impulsively asking her that night in front of the convenience store if she was Dr. Forester's wife. In a small town once you know who somebody is, you keep seeing them again and again.

I heard their voices, but not their words. They spoke intensely. When I slightly turned my head and glanced at them out of the corner of my eye, I saw that she looked anguished, brows knit together, eyes half-closed. I was convinced they were deeply involved, and felt sorry for Dr. Forester. Then I reminded myself I was deceiving him as well, and felt worse.

"You look flushed, Eva. Are you okay?" Bill asked. "Do you want to go home?"

He seemed preoccupied, and I assumed it was because of the business meeting. Usually he would tell me about it directly afterward, but he hadn't yet said a word. That meant he was either overly confident or terribly insecure about it. He enjoys discussing his work with me, and has said many times that he likes the way I look at things, that I'm pretty even-handed. I've always been this way with Bill—he brings it out in me. Until I met him, I never realized I could possess a calm, rational outlook.

"Yes, let's go," I said. I got up and headed toward the door.

Once we were outside the Inn I breathed a sigh of relief, knowing that Bill had either not seen Sam or had not recognized him. As I reached for Bill's hand, I said, "It's good to be walking. The bar felt stuffy and warm."

"It was your idea to meet there, Eva," he said nonchalantly, his eyes resting on a building under construction. He tilted his head, assessing what had been accomplished so far. He had a fine eye, aesthetic really, yet his nature was entirely practical. That practicality has allowed me to be relatively even-keeled these past thirty years.

"Bill, I'm restless. I think we should get away for a week or so."

"Sure Eva, let me see when—maybe a long weekend." He wasn't pleased with the idea of taking time off from work, especially now that the project was nearly finished. But I knew he'd be flexible for my sake. "You haven't said much about the new doctor you've been seeing this past month or so. Isn't that his office building across from the construction site?"

"Yes, that is his office. He's fine, Bill," I said, feeling uneasy.

"You don't seem to be as fearful of showering with the door closed as you used to be. It's funny to think about you having a fear, Eva. When did that start? I can't remember—it seemed to have happened all of a sudden, out of the blue. He must be helping you. So you like him—that's good."

I nodded, but didn't say more. My fear of water began once I discovered Dr. Forester was a psychiatrist in this town. Seeing his name on the building after we'd lived in Harrington for about a year had startled me.

When Bill and I returned home, I asked him to look at his schedule right away. I was beginning to feel anxious, and I wanted to make plans. I wanted to get away from Harrington not only for a week, but forever.

For many years my past has been creeping up behind me. In Harrington I have come to face it. Yet in doing so I've deceived not only Dr. Forester, but Bill as well.

Seventeen

Brea, late July

This morning Brea has decided to walk instead of drive; it is better to exercise when she's in this frame of mind. Stephen was restless in bed last night, and she's feeling moody from lack of sleep. She walks through the center of town toward the pool where she'll meet her son. At dinner last night Ned pleaded with her to come and see how fast he now swims. "Of course, darling," she'd said, "I'd love to." Stephen hadn't said anything, just sat there wearing that abstract expression of his, and she'd been annoyed—he should have shown interest in Ned's improved swimming.

It isn't too hot yet, she thinks, looking up at the hazy sky. As she comes near the gazebo, she notices a colored poster pinned to one column. Unusual, she thinks, a sign blemishing Harrington's pristine gazebo.

As she moves closer, she sees it's an advertisement for an upcoming fair. Ned will want to go, she thinks; it's been years since she's been to one.

Clearly she remembers a fair she went to when she was a few years younger than Ned. It was in Central Park, warm and close at dusk. Her mother was laughing with Mr. Vladimir, the neighbor they'd bumped into while in line at the hot dog stand. Silently agitated, Brea looked up at her father and pressed his hand, longing to see more of the fair.

Her mother laughed, looking steadily into Mr. Vladimir's eyes. Brea watched them as she stood beside her father, grasping his wrist. In her other hand, she held a paper cone with pink cotton candy, puffs of it sticking to her palms. She could hear the clanging, odd music of the merry-go-round, and was anxious to move on, feeling sick from her mother's laughter, her father's silence, his apparent lack of interest, not taking part in the conversation. And she was silently angry with her parents, the dishonesty brewing between them. She knew this from her mother's averted eyes when she spoke to her father, her look of distaste.

Now Brea reaches out. She wants to tear down the poster from the gazebo column, but stops herself. She thinks of Ned, and begins to walk in the direction of the pool.

That day at the fair she not only noticed the lack of honesty between her parents, she began to accept it as part of who they were, and eventually became resigned to it. She hadn't been surprised when a few years later they stood in front of her one early November evening before dinner, each parent taking one of Brea's hands, telling her they were going their separate ways. She was thirteen at the time, and because of her age and her sex she initially identified with her mother, not because she loved her more but because she felt it was more practical to do so. And her mother's failings were much easier for her to deal with than her father's. He was a quiet type, restrained.

She knows she's inherited something of Adele's sensuality, though her own is not as brusque or demanding as her mother's. Yet she's inherited her father's stoicism as well. She knows the side of her that's most like her mother has been dominant, ever since she, Stephen, and Ned returned from their spring trip to St. Lucia. Men hadn't seemed to notice her as much on the beach as in the past, something she'd previously taken for granted and had never before thought important. And so when she returned home she purchased summer dresses that perhaps were a little too revealing, she acknowledges.

She stops walking and presses her hand to her forehead. Yet she isn't completely like her mother. Her disciplined approach to her work—yes, she did get that from her father, she thinks. She does love him, and at times prefers his company. What she loves about him is his subdued but tenacious nature, which she finds soothing.

Once her parents were divorced, she longed to go to her father for comfort. She seeks the same sense of solace from Stephen. But something has changed, she thinks as she opens the gate to the pool; Stephen's become too preoccupied, too distant. And she is so very angry. She spots Ned, who with his friend is about to dive into the water. As she hurries toward him her heart pounds furiously.

Eva's Journal

After my divorce I frequented a bar, Salt Minds, not far from where I worked, close to the financial district in Boston. I felt more tranquil and solitary in a noisy environment than in a silent one. Although I did not go there for the express purpose of meeting someone—I went whenever I wanted to be alone—Salt Minds is where I met Bill.

At the time I had begun to take courses toward a graduate degree. And though I kept my job at the bank where I was an account manager, I found the work tedious. I was becoming more and more frustrated with all the paperwork. My English coursework was a welcome reprieve.

That night at the bar, I was twenty-seven years old and thinking seriously about what I should do next, whether I should quit my job and go to school full time or find another position. Life seemed an endless river and I was uncertain which tributary to follow.

Aunt Lora had become a subdued version of her old self. Although I would have been able to save money if I had, I didn't live with her after my divorce. I hadn't asked for a settlement from Richard. Given the circumstances, I didn't think it would have been right.

From time to time I'd visit Aunt Lora, and on the evening I met Bill I had just returned from seeing her. She'd been quite forlorn that evening, sitting in the dark talking about her husband and my father, and how much she missed them. I told her she was still in the prime of her life, and that she should move on. She must have been only a few years older than I am now and was still very attractive, her hair so blond and full.

She had no need to go on with her life now, she said, she preferred to remember—though I knew she still saw friends and made some efforts socially. Now she worked part time in a CVS store that once was a Woolworth's. When I left her that night, I knew I hadn't helped her feel less lonely. She was my only close relative, and I was fearful I would become like her, only thinking of the past, never really getting on with my life.

That night at the bar I thought about my future, wondered what it would be like to have children. Soon I felt someone come and sit next to me. Usually I was oblivious to others in the bar. Often I didn't even order a glass of wine—just a Coke or ginger ale. I liked the activity of the bar; it reminded me of sitting in the coat check room with Claudia at Happenings. I was able to relax—as I said, I liked the noise, it comforted me.

Perhaps it was Bill's scent that made me curious, clean and swift, like mint. Bill wasn't alone, so I didn't look at him for very long, but long enough to sense a calmness about him. He was with three or four other men, colleagues of some sort—obvious from the way they interacted—it was in an edgy, intimate way.

While Bill talked with a colleague, he had one hand on the back of my chair, and his head was turned away toward a man whom I'd come to know as Paul. They had a truly professional relationship—collegial. Paul nodded while he spoke, and I was intrigued by Bill's voice, low and persuasive—it struck a chord. He sounded like someone from the past, but I couldn't remember who. Rocco, I thought, the man my father worked for before becoming a musician. I was trying to remember Rocco's voice when Bill turned to me and asked if I was alone. I nodded, and then realized he wanted me to move over so Paul could sit in my seat.

I moved to a small table away from the bar, where I sipped from my glass of ginger ale and read the novel for my course on Henry James. There were only ten of us in the class. The professor had each of us choose one of James's novels, become an expert on it, and teach it to the class. Naturally I chose The Princess Casamassima—I also liked the working-class aspect of the novel.

It was late March, still quite cool. I wore a sweater, long skirt, and boots. Once I moved to the table, I thought it best to forget my plans for the future and con-centrate on the present. My next class was the following evening and I needed to read one hundred pages. Soon I was preoccupied with the novel, thinking about what I'd say about it in class, when I looked up and saw that Bill's friends had left, and he was alone. I returned to the novel and was startled some moments later when Bill came up to me. "I want to thank you for giving up your seat," he said. He stood gripping the back of the chair next to me, looking as if he regretted coming over.

"That's okay, I'm alone. I wasn't saving it for anyone." I said, slowly being drawn from the novel into the real world.

"Do you mind if I join you?" he asked. "Or do you prefer the company of Mr. James?" he inquired as he pointed to the book in my hands.

I smiled.

The waiter came over and after Bill ordered a drink, I told him my father was a jazz pianist who had played in a nightclub when I was a young girl, and that he and my mother had passed away some time ago, and that was why I liked to sit and read in this sort of atmosphere. I also said I was divorced.

He seemed surprised by my forthrightness, but answered in an even way, saying that it sounded as if things hadn't been easy for me.

Superficially his story was less complicated than mine. He was from the Midwest and had studied architecture at Tulane University. He'd been living in Boston for two years. His parents were still alive and quite active. He was the oldest of three brothers. He seemed almost embarrassed by his good fortune. But I wasn't naïve, and knew there was much more to him.

He saw I was hesitant, and didn't ask for my phone number or if I'd like a ride home that night. Would I be at the bar the next evening? he asked. I told him that I had a class the next evening, but I'd be there the night after that. His shoulders were broad, his physique solid, and he was tidy in a relaxed way. I thought longingly of Richard, my first husband. I hadn't been with another man since Richard. When I looked at Bill, I told myself I needed to put the past behind me.

I doubted I'd ever see him again. We seemed too reticent, each in our own way. Two evenings later, I returned but he wasn't there. I was a little late as I'd been stuck in traffic. I had taken a cab from my apartment and the driver had let me off two blocks from the bar. It was raining heavily, a cold, discouraging rain that had left my hair damp and clinging to my head unbecomingly. I looked like a long-haired castaway, I thought, when I caught my reflection in the mirror above the bar. Then I went and sat at the same table. Soon I gave up hope that Bill would come and became engrossed in The Princess Casamassima. Bill arrived about forty-five minutes later. By that time I was dry, my hair looked acceptable, and I felt warm and content, the cold having been erased from my body.

I felt his presence before I saw him. And when I looked up, he stood behind the same chair, gripping the back of it in the same way he had two nights before.

I motioned for him to sit down. When he saw that I was drinking a cup of hot coffee, he asked if I didn't drink alcohol.

"Occasionally," I said. "Rarely when I'm alone at a bar."

"I am here with you," he answered evenly.

I smiled. "But I don't know you, really. I know your name is Bill, and you're from Chicago. You studied architecture at Tulane, and work for a Boston architectural firm on State Street. I don't know more than that. Oh, yes, you're the oldest of three brothers. And your family is very normal." I said the word "normal" with a touch of irony.

He looked pleased.

After he ordered a glass of beer, he asked if I'd like to go to dinner. He realized it was a little late but he'd been detained at a meeting.

Something about the tone of his voice caused me to feel at ease. He got up as if I had said yes and soon we were on our way. I was glad the rain had let up. His car, an old BMW, was parked nearby.

Over dinner that evening and after two glasses of wine, I told Bill about Aunt Lora, what she was like before I went to live with her, before my parents had died. That Aunt Lora had lived a secretive life with her lover, and no one else had known except me, not even my parents.

I said I was the one who had helped her deceive those closest to her by going to her home every day after school to cover for her while she lived with her lover. Then I told him how one day I decided I was tired of taking care of Aunt Lora in this way. I didn't have friends, and felt older than my age. I had become too preoccupied with keeping her secret and so I concocted a plan to be free from her. What was most important was to be free, no longer weighed down by the adult world with all its intricacies, circumlocutions, and deceptions.

Bill was intrigued. At one point he interrupted, putting his hand over mine. "You sound guilty, Eva, and you shouldn't be. You were a child. You were not responsible. And even if you were partly responsible, you shouldn't carry guilt. Guilt is bad, bad, bad; it stops you from truly living." His eyes narrowed, and he spoke intensely, which surprised me.

I put my other hand on top of his. "What happened in your past, Bill? What happened that's so upset you? I know there's more to you. Life hasn't been that simple for you, it never is for anyone, really." I spoke earnestly because I liked him.

"Four years ago my father's brother killed himself. And I was the one who found him. We were a close family," Bill said, "but his death stymied us. Then we weren't as close anymore. There were many arguments, regrets, resentments. And I moved away because I didn't think they'd ever get over it, and I couldn't live with their guilt. Why did they feel guilty? To this day I don't know. I had to get away, and so I applied for jobs in other cities. Eventually I got a position in Boston."

I could see he didn't like talking about himself and soon turned the conversation to my story. "What about your plan, Eva? Were you able to extricate yourself from the situation?"

"My plan?"

"Was it successful?" he asked.

At that moment, it would have been natural for me to tell him about the circumstances of my parents' deaths, and how that got in the way of my plan. But I held back. I couldn't tell him the rest of my story either. Eventually I would tell him about my parents, and hint about what else had happened—you see, hinting was enough for Bill; he was quick and caught on without my having to explain. But I didn't tell him more that night; I only spoke of Aunt Lora.

"No, I would say my plan wasn't successful because it was aborted."

"Did your aunt stay with this man, her lover?"

"*For a while, but she left him, or he may have left her—I don't know. She never said and I didn't ask.*"

"*So were you free once she and her lover parted?*"

"*No, I became less free.*"

Eighteen

Brea, late July

The windows in Sam's office are wide open. Brea, sitting in a folding chair, welcomes the comforting breeze. Next to her is another cast member, Jared, who plays Mrs. Alving's son. Sam sits opposite them, at his desk, leafing through the script. She and Jared face him as if awaiting punishment.

Sam looks puzzled, his eyes narrowing; perspiration beads his forehead as he concentrates.

Brea looks over at Jared, who has pulled out his cell phone. His hair is thick and dark with traces of gray, though he is in his mid-thirties. His face a little swollen as if he hasn't slept much, she thinks.

Why is Sam doing this? Brea wonders. What is his point? Why doesn't he just say what is on his mind instead of treating them like schoolchildren while he acts officiously? Jared looks bemused, glancing at his large gold watch, and she too is impatient.

Abruptly Sam puts down the script and leans toward them. "We open in a week and I'm still not satisfied with what's happening. There's something not clicking. And I'm not certain why. It could be there's a hesitancy on both your parts—in your lines somewhat, but mostly in your body language, I think. The plot is simple, really, perhaps deceptively simple. A widow is having an orphanage built in memory of her husband, and it's overseen by the pastor, who had encouraged the widow, Mrs. Alving, to stay with her husband years before when she wanted to leave him because of his philandering. The son's come home to die as he has inherited "the disease," so to speak, from his father. The maid apparently is the illegitimate daughter of his father, and the son is falling in love with her. The mother is conflicted about helping her son die, and the orphanage burns down in a fire. It's the individual lines that are of utmost importance because they tell so much more than the story, which is straight-forward, but the dialog isn't—my interpretation, of course. I want the two of you to talk it over, stay in the office, see if you can work it out. It isn't terrible by any means, it's just not quite yet what it can be—perhaps it never will be in this production. Maybe I've got the chemistry wrong. I don't know. I'm going to lunch now."

Sam throws his hands up in the air. "It's just when something is this close to being excellent—it really is frustrating. I hope I'm not being hypercritical. After all, you're both strong intuitive actors!" With that, he waves good-bye and leaves the room in a flurry.

"Thanks a lot," Brea mutters.

"Brea, I think I know the problem," Jared says, sounding hesitant.

"What is it? Be straightforward."

"You don't seem like yourself—you're more impatient when we work through a scene. I'm having trouble responding to you."

Brea is stunned. Her heart pounds. She feels Jared's hand on her arm.

"Brea, stop being diverted. Become Mrs. Alving," he says quietly.

When she leaves the theater in the early evening, she feels a stillness, not knowing where to turn next. Although the late afternoon rehearsal had gone better than usual—even Sam seemed pleased—Jared was right. She's been diverted, diverted by her growing anger towards Stephen, her desire for Sam, and how hollow and spent she feels from it all.

She recalls the woman she saw in front of the convenience store who had asked if she were Dr. Forester's wife. Isn't that how she should be thinking of Mrs. Alving? Attractive in a mature way, emotionally strong, and yes, flawed, Brea thinks. As flawed as she is in her desire for Sam.

She checks her watch and sees it is time to pick up Ned from his baseball game. She's left her car in a parking space in the town center near the lingerie shop. When she reaches the car, her eyes fill, and before she gets in she looks up; through her tears she sees walking across the street the same woman she'd just been thinking of, the one who'd asked if she was Dr. Forester's wife. Tall and striking and so very well dressed, it would be difficult not to notice her. She is not smoking now, and her hair is swept off her face, held up with a barrette.

Brea sees the woman is looking straight ahead and doesn't notice her; she is approaching a man about her age, and when they meet their lips briefly touch, and then they walk hand in hand and go into the bookstore. There is something in her walk, Brea apprehends, the way her head is held high yet her shoulders droop—guilt. Yes, she feels guilty about something. Guilt—a feeling Brea is not familiar with, something she's never really understood. Mrs. Alving, Brea thinks; Mrs. Alving's sexuality is not unlike this woman's, wrapped up in feelings of guilt.

Eva's Journal

Earlier today, just past noon, I sat beside the pool at the hotel we've been staying in on Captiva Island, thinking how good it is to be away from New England where I feel more confined than in other places.

The swimmers floated by, the sun blazed down on them, and it was clear that my fear of water was lessening as I had chosen a chaise lounge very close to the edge of the pool.

Bill came toward me with, a gin and tonic in each hand, looking completely at ease in his blue bathing trunks and dark glasses.

At that moment I longed to tell him the truth about Dr. Forester. Bill sat on the chaise lounge next to mine. After placing the drinks on the table between our chairs, he pointed to the closed journal on my lap.

"Going to write about all your deep dark secrets?" he said in his matter-of-fact way.

"Bill," I said in protest, shaking my head.

"You look uneasy, Eva."

"I am, you know that, Bill. When we met, you told me guilt was a waste of time, but look how much time I've lost being guilty. I thought you had rescued me from it. All these years it's been there silent, yet present, ready to explode."

"Has it, Eva?"

"Bill," I said, pleading with him, "I need to be rescued again, all over again." I reached out to embrace him, and as I did so the journal fell off my lap, landing at the edge of the pool. I stood up. As I was about to reach for it, a young boy ran by, tipping the journal into the pool with his foot. I saw it floating, and without thinking I jumped into water to retrieve what I believed was my soul. I grasped it before it sank. And just as I did so, I realized Bill was in the water beside me. Tears were streaming down my face.

I didn't panic. My heart pounded; I was elated. And I held the journal in my hand, raising it high above my head.

"You've done it, Eva, you've done it!" Bill cried out, as I began to shake with relief.

While I wrapped myself in a towel, Bill studied the journal to assess the damage. "Looks like it's in fairly good shape, some pages are wet, though mostly legible, and should dry out okay. You may want to recopy parts of what you've written. So Eva, there goes your fear of water—I guess that psychiatrist has helped you."

I looked at Bill, felt so angry with him at that moment. But I knew in my crazy offbeat way, I loved him.

I put my arm around him and said, "Love me, Bill." And for an intense moment, he held me close, but just as quickly he drew away, and began talking about our son, Jesse, saying that he was concerned Jesse was taking too much on at work. "Has he spoken to you about it lately, Eva?" Bill asked.

I shook my head. Bill is the real mother in our family. I never clung to the children. I wanted them to have freedom, which was always high on my list of priorities.

Now I sit at the desk in our hotel room, gazing out the window at the setting sun casting an orange glow over the gulf. I toy with the idea of writing to Dr. Forester to tell him I no longer want to be his patient. I'm not good for him. We're not a match. It was folly to have gone to him in the first place. What was I trying to prove? I thought I'd discover the truth, but all I get from being with him is a hollow sense of revenge. It is becoming more and more difficult to witness his confusion and know it is partly because of me.

I know he's suffering—he just doesn't know why. I'm suffering too; he's not alone. But my suffering is more severe than his; I care for him as one human being cares for another in a catastrophe—it's as if we're together in a burning building.

Yet I know I'll return to him. Is it because of what happened to my parents? I wonder. As I think of them, the Van Gogh copy in Dr. Forester's waiting room comes to mind.

The last year of their lives, Father only played at Happenings; it seemed as if he didn't want to go any further with his music. Mother no longer booked him at different gigs. In her new role, she'd encourage people to come and hear him play, put advertisements in the newspaper, and so it seemed that Happenings would be their one and only chance for success. I wonder if they ever wanted more of a cut of the profits. It would not have been unreasonable because my father's playing brought in clientele from all over Boston, Providence, and even New York. People of all backgrounds, other artists, academics, businessmen, doctors, lawyers, were all curious to hear Ledo play, Ledo Morelli.

Someone from New York once came and offered him a permanent job, but he didn't take it—something kept him tied to Happenings. I don't know if it was a lack of confidence, or if he was compelled to stay there for some other reason. Yet he continued to play at Happenings and draw in customers, customers who were willing to spend a good deal to eat and drink, and to listen to Ledo.

Nineteen

Maybe Harrington isn't so bad after all, Brea thinks. She's standing out on the deck sipping at a cup of coffee. The backyard is pleasant this morning—beautiful really, the oak in one corner, tall and expansive, and despite the heat, the grass isn't parched but a bright and vibrant green. She sighs. Ten days left of *Ghosts*. On one hand she longs for the play to end so she can go off to Italy and hopefully resolve things with Stephen; on the other, she doesn't wants *Ghosts* to stop because at last she finds the character of Mrs. Alving compelling. Her words resonate, reach out to Brea, captivating her.

Last week her mother came to a performance. Afterward, as they sipped drinks out on the deck, Adele leaned her head back into her chair and studied her daughter with wily eyes. "You and Sam work well together—you anticipate one another." Her mother's words flowed into the stillness of the hot summer night, lingering, like the sound of the crickets. Brea wanted to lash out, remind her mother that she was an actress—of course she and Sam would anticipate one another on stage. But she remained silent.

Brea wishes Stephen would not wait for the last performance to see the play as he usually does. She very much wants him to see it. Maybe it will capture his attention, bring him back to her. It's as though he's been away this summer. And her anger about his absence hasn't remedied the situation.

Her thoughts float to the first time they made love. They'd been seeing one another for a month, and she wondered why nothing had happened sooner. She wasn't convinced it was because he'd been paged at the most inopportune times. More than likely it was because of his cautious nature. He hadn't wanted to overwhelm her. Later he said he'd revealed too much about himself too soon—he was concerned he may have bored her. To the contrary; she'd found him to be refreshingly real, solid and humane. And that first time they'd had coffee together was when she'd fallen in love with him.

She remembers his expression when he came into her apartment that night, a month after they'd met. He was sheepish and expectant, and she'd been charmed—oh so charmed. There was nothing of the detached lover about him, or the self-centered one. He was thoughtful and caring, and honest. Tears come to her eyes.

Why has he been so preoccupied this summer? she asks again. It must be Florence—or maybe he no longer desires her, doesn't love her as much.

For a moment she feels lost. When she is more composed, her thoughts rush to her work, and to Sam—he is much more professional than she'd believed. If only she had known what a talented actor he is, it would have made her less dissatisfied with Harrington and its theater.

She recalls the night of the first performance. When the play was over, Sam had taken her aside and had whispered in her ear that she had indeed become Mrs. Alving. And she had answered in a steady voice that it was because she now understood guilt. Then he hugged her so tightly she didn't want him to let go. Her performance that evening had been more successful than she would ever have imagined just a few weeks before.

As she thinks of Sam, she feels a sharp pang, a longing that is causing her more anguish than ever. But she'll force herself to remain loyal to Stephen— there's no other way. What is happening? she wonders, shaking her head—just jitters, she thinks, jitters about the closing in two weeks of *Ghosts*—separating from Mrs. Alving—and Sam.

Eva's Journal

A few days after Bill and I returned from Captiva, I went to see Dr. Forester. When I walked into his office, I announced I could now swim in a pool without being afraid. He didn't seem surprised, had a wry look on his face as if he didn't quite believe me, or thought I hadn't been honest from the start.

He is supposed to be a mirror, reflecting the emotions I show him—that is the way it should work. But in my case, maybe I'm the mirror reflecting back to him what he doesn't want to see or is unable to see because the glass is opaque.

We didn't spend much time discussing why my fear of water had passed. I was disappointed he didn't say more about it. Instead he asked if Aunt Lora had ever taken me to a beach or a pool.

Before I knew it, I was speaking about her, and revealed more than I intended to.

"You covered for your aunt Lora?" He spoke as if he were questioning himself more than me. "That was quite an undertaking for a young girl."

"Yes, but I loved her. She'd been so kind to me. I'd do anything she asked. She was the only person I could depend on. My parents were so wrapped up in my father's playing at Happenings. It was such a depressing place, and I believed Aunt Lora didn't like it there either. But I did appreciate that my father played so wonderfully. I just could no longer go to hear him perform at the nightclub. It was more than Uncle Mario's death; there'd always been something dark and sinister about Happenings."

"Were you frightened when you went there?"

"I was fearful of the people who made a point of speaking with my mother. They bothered me. Other people who ate there, and listened to my father's music, they seemed quite harmless. But yes, I was frightened by those who came over to my mother."

"Did your mother seem frightened?"

"I never considered that. My mother wasn't a particularly beautiful woman, not as stunning as Aunt Lora was, but she would light up when she spoke to certain people and she'd become very attractive. I must admit I was proud of her at those moments, elated. Now I think, how shallow of me."

"Well, that's not unusual for a young girl to want her mother to appear attractive. That's natural. It has to do with pride in your mother, needing to feel good about her. You shouldn't be hard on yourself because of that."

"But don't you see, Doctor—all these things add up and make me feel guilty because of how my parents died."

"*Please go on, Mrs. Hathaway,*" *he said. He sat more erectly now, his legs crossed. His expression was gentle, yet his gaze was direct and impassive.*

I looked at him and attempted to smile, but felt pained by of all that had happened. And he saw how quickly my smile turned into a frown, and very soon I was in tears.

I took one of the tissues from the box on the table next to my chair and wiped away my tears. When I felt composed, I said, "I don't remember if I stopped in at Aunt Lora's the day they died. But I was on my way home, walking down the street. It was an early April day, breezy, but the sky was a clear blue and the air was surprisingly warm." He nodded, and I continued slowly, not wanting to omit any details. "As I walked closer, I saw police cars with flashing lights. And I froze. In synchrony, the neighbors hastily came out to the street, and I began to run toward my home. When the woman who lived next door saw me, she threw her arms around me, hugging me, preventing me from moving any closer to the police cars. Her eyes were filled with tears. She told me that Aunt Lora would be coming soon. The woman wore a red and yellow flowery dress. But I don't recall her name, only her dress—how silly of me to remember that."

I stopped talking for a while, covered my face with my hands, and took a deep breath before telling more.

"*Soon I realized she was not letting go, was trying to block my view. Then I overheard people talking and the words 'murder-suicide.' I screamed and broke free from the woman's embrace. I ran until I was stopped by a policeman, who told me I couldn't go any farther. I told him I lived there, pointing to my home and crying uncon-*

trollably. Then I felt a hand on my shoulder, and I turned round and saw Aunt Lora. Tears were streaming down her face."

Now I looked directly at Dr. Forester, noticing he had turned pale, his mouth was opened, and his eyes misty.

"Aunt Lora told the policemen who we were, and I insisted on seeing my parents. After a few minutes, we learned from the detective that my parents had already been taken away. At that moment Aunt Lora fainted; I felt her foot against mine as she lay on the ground. The woman in the red and yellow dress helped revive her, and we went inside her home. Eventually we were given sedatives, but I don't know by whom; it's all a blur.

"That night I slept with Aunt Lora in her bed, my arms wrapped around her. I remember how still she lay, her body turned away from mine. Eventually I fell asleep. When I awoke the next morning, my first thought was that it had all been a dream.

"During breakfast we did not speak to one another; we just looked down at the food on our plates we hardly touched. After we finished eating, Aunt Lora stood up, came to me and held me in her arms. She told me that it appears as if my father shot my mother in the back in their bedroom. She may have been taking a nap. Then he shot himself in the heart."

Dr. Forester didn't say anything. He waited for me to say more, but I was exhausted and didn't speak for a while. "It was ruled a murder-suicide, but I always thought there was more to it than that. My parents were loyal to one another. A murder-suicide often implies a lover, but I'm certain neither of them had a lover. It was such a tragedy, Dr. Forester. Yet it's all in the past. I *can't bring them back; I tried to for years. I'd imagine them living in the house that Aunt Lora had sold, working at Happenings, though I never went near the nightclub; I don't even know how long it remained in business."*

"Yes, Eva," he said, his pale green eyes deeply saddened. "It's very tragic, for you, for them. Your father drank. You've said he was drinking excessively, and he became aggressive when he drank. Maybe they were having an argument about his drinking, or money, and your mother became exhausted from it and fell asleep. I don't know, Eva, and you don't either. You could not have prevented what happened, even if you knew the truth about what was bothering them. You must realize that so you can free yourself of all the guilt."

"But you see, Doctor, there are other reasons I feel guilty that I can't discuss with you. You must understand this."

At that moment our gazes met, and I saw his unease. How pleading and desperate I must have appeared. He turned away and opened his laptop. Then he looked at me again, his eyes now impassive. He asked when I could see him next, and I noticed a slight quiver cross his lips.

Twenty

Stephen, early August

Stephen drives south toward Boston in the third of four lanes on I-95. It's over ninety degrees; he wipes perspiration from his forehead. His shirt feels moist, yet he refrains from turning on the air conditioning; he finds the steady stream of hollow air more discomforting than the steamy weather. He thinks how little sleep he's had since Mrs. Hathaway told him about her parents' murder-suicide.

As he takes the exit onto Route 1, he reviews what he'll say to Philip, how he'll describe his concerns about Eva Hathaway. What bothers him most is he doesn't know in which direction the therapeutic relationship is heading. It's as if, for no logical reason, he can't extricate himself from the churning waters of a whirlpool that initially seemed harmless.

He's mentioned to her countless times that she should go see someone else, that he could refer her to another therapist. Would she prefer a woman? Her refusal is always strong and definite, but a look of subdued fright crosses her face as if she's about to lose something quite dear to her. At the same time she never appears offended by his suggestion. It's as though she's made up her mind that he's the doctor for her, and no one else will do. How can she be so certain? he wonders. She doesn't appear to have an emotional connection to him.

As he makes his way through the heavy traffic in Boston, nearly driving through a red light on Beacon Street, it occurs to him that she may be lying on some level, but he isn't one to evaluate a patient by his or her exact words or stories. A case invariably involves certain facts, but he's always been more interested in nuance, the impression he gets about the patient from the tone of his or her voice or body language—literal truth has never been important in his success at treating a patient, in his ability to diagnose. Listening to a patient's words is like listening to a patient's heart through a stethoscope—the same exacting, sensitive ear is needed.

He begins to wonder if in this case, his past suppositions don't apply. As his writings on the subject of listening suggest, he may not be hearing her as he should—how ironic, he thinks. This case is an intellectual puzzle, much more so than any other—or it might be his imagination, or even worse, his emotions running away from him.

Philip has left open the door to his main office. And so when Stephen enters the waiting room, he sees

Philip in the adjoining room, at his desk, reading from his computer. His hair is long and now completely gray. When he looks up and sees Stephen he smiles, then stands and comes forward to shake his hand. He looks older, Stephen thinks, not certain exactly how much older Philip is than he—maybe twelve or fifteen years.

"You're looking well, Stephen," Philip says, touching his own face with his hand, to show he notices Stephen's light tan. He motions for him to come into his inner office. "So you have come about a patient?"

"Yes, but of course it's always good to see you, Philip."

Philip, who has been studying Stephen, sits in his chair. "How is Brea?" he asks nonchalantly.

"Fine, she's playing Mrs. Alving in *Ghosts* this summer."

"I like Ibsen, and I'd like to see her. I hear she's good, very good, in fact. My wife went to one of her performances a few years ago when she was at a conference in Manchester."

"You never told me," Stephen answers, somewhat surprised. And Stephen thinks of Brea's difficulty connecting with the role of Mrs. Alving. He remembers how he used to be annoyed and a bit jealous when she came upon a role she didn't quite feel comfortable with and as a result would be a little bit distant from him and distracted from their marriage. But never had she been as enigmatic as she is now.

Stephen leans back in his chair, letting his guard down as he does with those to whom he feels close. He speaks in a more expansive and emphatic way than he normally does. "Philip, I have this patient. I just cannot get a grip on her. Her diagnosis is pretty straightforward, but I am convinced I am missing something."

"Stephen," Philip says in exasperation. "What about something as basic as countertransference—hasn't that crossed your mind?"

Stephen looks directly at Philip. "Yes, of course, Philip. I've asked myself if she reminds me of someone. But I don't know who that could be. Initially she did remind me of a babysitter I had for a few years when I was a child, but the more I get to know her, the less like this woman she seems, and now the resemblance is fleeting at best."

In an exacting tone, his voice low, Stephen gives Philip his description, her general age, her situation, her reason for coming to him.

"Murder-suicide—that's pretty grim—must have been devastating for her," Philip says when Stephen finishes. "How long ago was that?" He stands up and turns away to pour a cup of coffee for Stephen from the coffee maker behind his desk.

"She was sixteen at the time—it must have happened in the mid- to late sixties," Stephen says, and notices Philip's back stiffen as if something has just occurred to him.

"Her aunt was more of a figure in her life than either of her parents. Her mother was not a particularly warm or encouraging person. She was mostly wrapped up in her husband's career, and goodness knows what else. Maybe she was having an affair—hence the murder-suicide. But my patient claims her parents were loyal to one another. And her father—I know she loved him, adored him, admired him as a musician—but as I said, he was an alcoholic, scattered and not able to focus any love on her. Now if her aunt had been involved in a tragic event, maybe she'd have been even more traumatized. If she'd lost her aunt, I believe she would have become deeply depressed. But she was angry with her parents, angry because they weren't attentive to her. So she feels deeply guilty about their deaths. And the truth is, Philip, I'm uneasy in her presence. Yes, my manner is professional, but it's a façade, a charade of sorts. I'm unable to view her objectively—it's as if she's a cousin, older by eight to ten years."

Philip turns around and meets his gaze, giving him a solemn look. Stephen feels taken aback. It is as if Philip pities for him for some reason.

"What is it, Philip—what are you thinking? Your mind seems to be steaming ahead, but you're not saying anything. Are you hiding something from me?" Stephen asks, his voice demanding.

"I do not hide, and only speak when I know the facts. As you know in certain instances, facts are essential. I suggest you send this patient to someone else," Philip says quietly, looking away. "You're missing something, Stephen, through no fault of your own; this happens to all of us from time to time. We all have our blind spots—this is yours."

"Oh, come now, Phil," Stephen says, baffled. "I've tried to send her to someone else, but she won't leave."

"Sometimes that happens, Stephen." He speaks firmly. "Eventually she'll leave you—you just have to see it through."

Eva's Journal

Have I fooled Dr. Forester? Or am I the fool? Now whenever I'm in a session with him, I try and hold his gaze, want him to know there's more to my story, more than I can tell. I bend forward in the chair as if I am about to explode with the information. But he's unflappable. He listens and questions me in his steady way, remaining impassive. And still he calls me Mrs. Hathaway—only occasionally he says Eva, but not if he can help it. I'm Eva to him—he should know that. If he knew the truth, he'd understand why I'm Eva to him. I'm not the distant Mrs. Hathaway, but the familiar Eva, the all-too-familiar Eva.

Bill knows what happened to me following the death of my parents. I told him slowly, over time, never misleading him, always letting him know there was more. From my experience with my first husband, I learned it is best not to reveal everything at once. Yet with Bill it might not have mattered.

"People are human," I said to Bill, explaining my first husband Richard's response. We'd been married then for about five years. We were driving out to Chicago to visit his family, our two children asleep in the back seat of the car. "You see, I hadn't been truthful from the start—and so he didn't really know what to believe or what not to believe. Richard was, and always has been a purist."

Bill shrugged and said, "Maybe you're right, Eva. But you defend him. You still love him some." He had a pained and distant look in his eyes as he gazed out at the road before him.

Over the years Bill has been patient because he loves me. Our children can tolerate only so much; Bill has always understood me. He's more aware of the limitations of people. Though now in their twenties, our children expect so much from those who are older; they want perfection or something close to it. Someday my relationship with them will improve; someday they'll appreciate me, as in my way I've always loved them.

But now the question is what to do with Dr. Forester—what do I say to him? Do I tell all? He's a kind person. I must tell him the truth. He's carrying a burden he's not aware of. His job is to free me, but it is I who must free him. I am responsible because I have deceived him. At first I was self-righteous, needing to even the score. I knew there was a dark side to what I was attempting, and that I had lost part of myself in going to him, but I thought that to be secondary, that I would regain myself through the process. Now I know the only way to return to my former self, my whole self, is to reveal the truth—it's the only way.

Last night I confessed to Bill why I went to see Dr. Forester. He stood at the foot of the bed, and looked down as I spoke. When I caught his gaze, he briefly studied me as if he didn't know me. But soon he came over to me. "You need help, Eva," he said, his hands cupping my shoulders. "But you've gone to the wrong person."

"I believed he was the right person, maybe the only person," I insisted.

"We should have discussed it—this idea of yours. You were both defiant and misguided in going through with it, Eva. I must be honest with you."

"You've always been honest with me, Bill. I don't disagree, but I was compelled to go to him. Now I must correct what's happened. I must free him."

"How will you do so?"

"I'll tell him."

Bill nodded and said, "As long as you tell him the truth, he'll be able to help you—that's all that matters."

"Do you despise me?"

"I can't. Maybe I should want to, but I can't." There were tears in his eyes. He held me very close.

When he released me, I said, "I'll let him know. I promise."

Twenty-One

Brea, mid-August

When Brea awakens, the sun is shining brightly, preventing her for a moment from seeing. As she shades her eyes with one hand, she looks over at the bedroom clock on the nightstand. It is nearly ten o'clock. She shakes her head in disbelief; she rarely sleeps in this late. Still in a haze, it takes her some time to realize that tonight will be the last performance of *Ghosts.*

Tomorrow she and Stephen will drive Ned to New York where he'll stay with her mother, and then they'll be off to Florence. She feels a sense of joy and longing—a childlike excitement. But she's so sleepy the feeling is muted and distant—she hasn't caught up with it yet, she acknowledges.

She wants to call Stephen, say something to him to lessen the tension. Does he have a patient now? she wonders and stops herself from picking up the phone.

Ned has spent the night at his friend Ross's house. He's told her that Ross's parents have separated, and so Ross wants to spend more time with Ned. That is understandable, she thinks. Though beginning tomorrow, Ned will be in New York for the remainder of the summer. She gets out of bed, puts on her light robe and starts to tie the belt. But because it is hot, she lets it hang loose over her sheer nightgown. She should get dressed, she thinks, but first she needs a cup of coffee.

As she shuffles down the stairs to the kitchen, the doorbell rings. She thinks it might be Ned, but remembers that he and Ross will be going to the pool and will stay there until early afternoon.

When she reaches the foot of the stairway, she goes to the side window, and peeks out. "Sam," she says groggily, but her heart pounds as she opens the door.

She is surprised to see him looking so forlorn. His eyes no longer appear hard and swirling, but soft and pleading. She feels a strong sense of anticipation. He doesn't say anything to her. She turns away and he follows her inside.

She wants to be free of her physical longing for him. When they go into the sitting room, she feels his hand on her shoulder, and her heart thumps so loudly she's certain Sam can hear it. He takes her hand, and they both sink into the plump cushions of the sofa, not uttering a word. There is only silence, except for the sound of her thumping heart, which doesn't comfort her—it is as if it's about to burst through her chest.

Sam slowly slips off her sheer robe. The straps of her negligee fall down past her shoulders. And when she rests her head back against the arm of the sofa, she feels his lips on her throat. With the tips of his fingers he caresses her eyes, her nose, her lips.

Although she is excited by his touch, she longs to push him away, to tell him to leave in her firm, theatrical voice. Vaguely she envisions herself running away from him, but her body is responding readily to his touch. He undresses her, kisses her navel, her breasts. Then she reaches out and presses her lips to his mouth.

When it is over and he is gone, her heart sinks. "Stephen," she calls out, her voice resonating like the cry of a seagull. Then she feels a darkness within her—such a darkness.

Twenty-Two

A little past ten in the morning and Stephen already feels the temperature rising, promising another hot day. Mrs. Hathaway is uncharacteristically late, he thinks, and pictures her sitting in the waiting room, her head erect, her shoulders languid, her large blue-gray eyes fixed on the copy of the Van Gogh painting. He shakes this image away, wonders if she's canceled and for some reason he has not received the message. He leaves his inner office door open so she'll know to come straight in.

As this evening is the closing night of *Ghosts,* he's restless. Anticipating Brea's performance makes him so, he knows. And in twenty-four hours they'll drive Ned to New York to his grandmother's, and then he and Brea will fly off to Florence. There's so much to do in a short amount of time. He begins to pace.

When he hears the outer door open, he immediately goes into the waiting room. Mrs. Hathaway, her eyes darting, stands in the doorway.

"Please come in."

"I know I'm late. I nearly didn't come," she says, passing him as she strides into his office and sits down in the swivel chair across from his desk.

"If you were in the middle of something, something unexpected, you could have called and canceled."

"No, I wasn't in the middle of anything. The truth is I wasn't certain if I wanted to see you again. We'll be moving to Boston in a few weeks. Bill's work here will be finished . . . but that isn't the reason I won't be coming again."

"I've always said, Mrs. Hathaway—it's your prerogative," he says, feeling a sense of loss.

As if something has occurred to her, she suddenly rises from the chair.

"Please have a seat," he says.

She ignores him and stands close to his desk. "I have deceived you," she says decidedly.

"Honesty isn't required in my office," he says. "And there are different kinds of honesty, honesty with words, and also there is honesty with feelings or what is being said between the words. I never take anyone at face value. If I did, I wouldn't be really listening. Would I?"

"I understand. But it is much more than that. When you know who I am, you will view me very differently."

"Essentially you are an honest person, Mrs. Hathaway. I will never think otherwise."

"I've learned over the course of this summer that you're a good person, Dr. Forester, honorable, and that's a rare quality—well, in my life at least. I haven't known goodness before. "

"But there's your husband, Mrs. Hathaway. From what you've said, he is an earnest, straightforward person."

"Yes, Bill is good, but I mean before Bill, much before Bill."

"When you were in your teens you lost your parents in a very tragic way. But you had your aunt."

"My aunt was better than most, but far from perfect."

"She may have prevented you from fully realizing your adolescence, but she was there for you—the one person who was there for you when you were growing up—not that your parents didn't love you. I'm certain they did."

"I know. Of course, it's impossible to know the true story of my parents. I can only speculate. That's not what's most important; it's the emotion their very tragic deaths evoked—that's what's paramount, and I hid from those feelings for so many years until I could no longer do so. And it was all expressed in my being dishonest with you—it's all very clear to me now, the details aren't important. If I hadn't made myself into a seemingly brave and diligent person, I'd have felt more. I'd have suppressed less, and I wouldn't have been burdened with so much fear and the need to seek revenge. I chose to put on a brave front—it was the thing to do—to forget the past. But it's caught up to me—the horror," she says, placing her hand over her heart. "I must go."

"I'm glad you came today, Mrs. Hathaway, Eva, even if it is the last time," Stephen says, thinking of Philip Barone's words: *Eventually she will leave you— you just have to see it through.*

He goes over to the door and opens it for her. As they shake hands, he notices how penetrating her gaze is.

He listens to her departing footsteps until he can no longer hear them. As he looks across the room, he sees that she's left her brown silk scarf on the chair. She always wears a scarf, even in the hot weather. He picks it up, holds it in both of his hands and feels how soft it is, how undulating. Brown—the same color as the dress in his memory. Who was he with that day in the dress shop on Newbury Street? He isn't convinced it was his mother; most likely it was Mrs. C., his babysitter. Brown, he says softly, the color, his feel-ings, his father's intellectualism, his mother's passion, and Mrs. C.'s earthiness. He'd been angry with the three of them. It's all so simple, yet at the same time most complex—what isn't said, he thinks bemusedly.

When he goes over to his desk, he notices a large envelope on his desk addressed to him. He sees Mrs. Hathaway's name in the upper left hand corner. That's strange, he thinks. He did not see her put it down. It must have been in her pocketbook—she always carries that large one with the gold buckle. She must have left it on his desk when he turned away from her to open the office door.

He unfastens the clip and pulls out the contents, pages ragged at the left edge as if they'd been ripped out of a notebook. The top of the first page reads: *Eva's Journal.* He glances at the next few lines. For a moment he feels a pulse of anxiety. He sits down to steady himself. His next patient has canceled. If he chooses, he can look over her journal now. But does he so choose? He briefly wonders about this, then sits back in his chair and begins to read.

Eva's Journal

These pages are for you, Dr. Forester. My hand trembles as I write.

It was nearly a year ago, a brisk late fall afternoon, when I noticed your name on the sign outside your office building. The opening of a clothing store across the square brought me to your street. Not until then did my rage and pain re-surface.

From my time with you I have gained some insight. I'm only beginning to understand what my life's been about, and I know it will take some time to truly comprehend what's happened to me. You helped me realize the depth of my pain—a pain I've been denying for many years. In the past I'd kept a distance from it, looked upon certain events in my life as if they were figments of my imagination, exaggerations; that was, until I saw your name, and started to see you.

During our sessions you began to know me, but in a certain sense you didn't know me at all. It was because

I was hiding from you, hiding my true self. I suppose most people go to you, hiding parts of themselves, but in most cases the hiding isn't purposeful. They come to you so you can reflect back to them what they are hiding. They know something is amiss in their lives, but aren't certain what it is or what they're hiding from. The opposite was true for me. Before I saw your name, I believed that for the most part there was nothing really amiss in my life—yes, I had experienced trauma in my youth—my parents' tragic deaths, etc., but I believed I was a relatively happy woman. Yes, relatively happy, but not content.

When I was fifteen, I had a plan, a childish one at that. Yet most plans are childish in the sense that when you construct them you believe they will be carried off without any hitches. The afternoon my parents died is when I forgot about my plan.

Before my parents' deaths, my plan had been to secretly discover the identity of Aunt Lora's lover. Little did I know at the time that my parents probably would not have minded if Aunt Lora had a friend, a married lover. Most likely they preferred that I stopped by Aunt Lora's house every day to keep me at a distance from whatever was occurring in their lives. It may have been because of my father's drinking or for another unknown reason. Despite their passion for one another, had one of them fallen in love with another person? I'll never know the truth. Over time I've realized that whether one of them had a lover, or whether it was because of my father's alcoholism, it didn't matter because it had to do with their compulsions and their inability to control themselves. Whatever the reason, who they were as individuals, and even more importantly who they were as a couple was very much the cause. But this hasn't been the only issue in my life. Their deaths were shocking and traumatic, but there was more, more because of when and how it occurred. You may wonder what was so devastating.

When my parents died, naturally I moved in with Aunt Lora. She'd become more forlorn, even more so than after her husband's death. The combination of her husband and her younger brother's untimely deaths had been almost too much for her to bear. And so, despite my own sorrow, I hoped to divert her. I desperately needed her to be as she was—the only person I could depend on and trust not only for practical support, but for emotional sustenance as well.

There should be no secrets between us now, I told her. Then I asked to meet the friend she lived with during the week. She looked at me quite seriously, and her melancholy seemed to evaporate. She became earnest. "Yes, Eva, I think it would be a good idea. You've been through so much for someone so young." Tears filled her hazel eyes, yellow and brown flecked, warm. "My friend is a doctor, someone you can speak with. Don't think of him as my friend, but as someone who can help you. I've spoken to him about all that's happened to you. You must go to him, Eva. I insist."

She must have sensed my reluctance once I realized he was a doctor because she repeated, "I insist. You must go. He's very good, someone who can help you with your sadness."

I was surprised by what she said, and I couldn't answer for a while. I hugged her and told her I tried not to think about what had happened. I wanted to remember the happy times I'd had with my parents, Father practicing the piano, sitting in my mother's lap, listening to him play, feeling secure in her arms. I only wanted to recall memories that were pleasing.

She appeared worried, and then she spoke to me as if I were a child. "Eva, I understand, but you must realize what has happened."

"I can't," I cried out. "I do not believe my father killed my mother. It is not possible!"

Tears ran down Aunt Lora's face as I spoke.

"I don't want to talk to your doctor friend," I said indignantly.

Then she turned away from me, and spoke quietly, "You must, Eva, you must."

I went alone to the appointment. Given her relationship to him, it wasn't appropriate for her to accompany me. He had a wife and a child, and was an intensely busy man, committed to his work. His wife was often away during the week.

I remember how my heart thumped as I rode the trolley to his office. It was in Boston, in Kenmore Square, in an old brick and stone building with Oriental carpeting, gold antique fixtures, and high ceilings. As I walked up the stairway, I gripped the banister tightly. Because other doctors—pediatricians, gynecologists, internists—were in the building, I smelled rubbing alcohol. The smell bothered me; it seemed like a warning not to go forward. But I'd always obeyed Aunt Lora, and so I went up to his office. I shook off any doubts because I trusted my aunt.

He was dressed in a very fine navy-blue suit, silk, I think, and his tie was a pale yellow silk as well; his hair was dark and smooth, brushed away from his solemn face. I'd never known anyone like him before, his grace and determination so inextricably linked. Yet at the same time he seemed quite familiar to me. He sat in a high-backed leather chair and his desk was low with four spindly legs. I sat before him in an embroidered armchair. He spoke in a calm way as if he had all the time in the world to listen—he wanted me to tell him about myself. I did so, hesitantly at first. But the more I went to him, the more forthcoming I became.

One day he suggested I lie on the couch. His voice was appeasing. He possessed a sense of dignity, I thought, the way he walked, his head slightly bent, his body thin and agile.

The first time I lay on his couch, I fell asleep, and I remember waking up and seeing him still sitting patiently in the chair, though he'd moved it closer to the couch.

"I'm sorry," I said, raising my head, realizing I had slept through most of the session. "I'm sorry for wasting your time."

"My time is never wasted," he assured me.

The next time I went to him, I spoke quickly and fully. I wanted to compensate for having fallen asleep during the last session. My words tumbled out—about my love for Aunt Lora, and how she'd been kinder to me than my parents had. But, I told him, my parents were different before Father played at Happenings. Happenings changed our life because it changed my parents. It was almost too much for them; it made them too excited, emotional and disorganized. Then I told him it was there my father had begun to drink.

The doctor's room was mostly dark, and when I spoke I looked up at the ceiling. The lights were low.

When I went to him in the late afternoon or early evening, it was easier to talk as it seemed quieter at those times, with no other patients in the waiting room.

I said how I'd loved to hear my father practice at the community center, and how I'd sit with my mother and listen to him. Although the floor of the auditorium was cold, his music kept me warm. All I wanted now, I told him, was to feel the same sense of warmth, closeness. As I spoke, tears rolled down my cheeks. What happened? I asked excitedly. Where are they? I cried out.

He didn't say anything, but I felt his reassuring hand on my shoulder. When he spoke I could not see his expression, because of the darkness. Sometimes I wasn't certain if he were there in the room with me.

Each time I went to him, I would lay on the couch and he would touch me more: first my face, then during a later session my arms and legs. Then it was my breasts, my vagina; he'd touch me until I'd cry out with pleasure, yet at the same time I'd never known such pain, I believed.

You see, Dr. Forester, it was Aunt Lora, Lora Casamassima, who took care of you while your mother was away. You called her Mrs. C.

I stopped seeing Dr. Arthur Forester when his relationship with Aunt Lora ended. I don't know how it ended or who ended it. I never told Aunt Lora what happened during my sessions with your father. Because she loved him, she would have been devastated. After their affair was over, she seemed to lose energy, her enthusiasm for living; she became a shell of her former self. And so I forgave her; I never doubted her love for me.

A few years ago, before she passed away, she told me one day out of the blue that she had stopped going to Happenings because she wanted to avoid your father. Your parents called him Mr. Green, she said. Do you remember, Eva? But then Mario died, she continued, and didn't say more.

I hated your father for what he did to me. I did not choose to go to him; I went because I trusted my aunt. I had no one else.

Twenty-Three

Brea, late August

Brea, at the window of the hotel room, gazes at the Ponte Vecchio, people milling about, and then the Arno River. In the distance she spots the Duomo. How old and dignified Florence is, she thinks. When she takes a few steps back, she notices her reflection in the mirror next to the window, her narrow face and wide mouth. She frowns. "I am not Anna Karenina, nor am I Emma Bovary," she says aloud—only too aware that her nature is neither romantic nor melancholic. Then she moves close to the window again, looking out, fingering the embroidered drapes.

Her heart beats rapidly—she is waiting for Stephen, who by now, she thinks, must have finished his presentation. Although he has not said anything to her, she's convinced he knows about her and Sam. When he came up to her after her closing night performance in Harrington, she had seen a look of hurt and anger on his face.

She knew he wouldn't bring it up until he was finished with his talk. That was his way, slow and methodical—while she longed for it to be out in the open. Yet as anxious as she'd been to get it over with, she hadn't wanted to distract him from his presentation. He'd worked too long and diligently on it.

So for these past five days she has, so to speak, held her breath. It has seemed more like two years to her, the waiting, the not knowing. What will she say? That she had not run away; she had accepted Sam— she had not shut the door on him. And because of this, is her marriage over? She takes a deep breath— no, that is impossible, she thinks. Tears spring to her eyes. She hears a sound and turns away from the window. Is it Stephen? Someone is opening the door to the room next to theirs. How much longer must she wait for him? Her throat feels constricted, her pulse quickens.

Twenty-Four

Stephen, late August

"The attributes of listening may be likened to a psychiatric condition—it is a physical, emotional, and environmental phenomenon. And once this is realized, the practitioner will be able to put him- or herself in the shoes of the patient," Stephen says to a quiet audience. He is unable to decipher the expressions on their faces.

A hand shoots up. Stephen nods at a somewhat scruffy-looking man in his early thirties, who stands and says he is a graduate student in psychology.

"Dr. Forester," he asks in English, his Italian accent light and endearing. "Is there any other part of your body you listen with, other than the ear?"

Unwittingly Stephen thinks of Eva's journal. Had his father been listening to Eva with his hands? Or had it been transference on her part, and he hadn't touched her at all? Or had his father willed Eva to believe he was touching her, because on a primitive level he'd been listening to her needs?

He notices passion in the student's eyes. Then he looks away and tells the audience that there are times when you must physically turn away from a patient so that he or she will see you are not hovering, and thus will feel more at ease. And so he supposes you can say that is called listening with your back. It is his attempt to use humor to deflect the question. And there is laughter, slight but sincere.

Now, having finished his presentation, he checks his watch and sees that it is only eleven a.m. He thinks of Eva Hathaway. When he finished reading her journal that day, he wrote her a letter. Since she was moving to Boston he referred her to Philip Barone. Walking down the stone steps of the university, the sun beating down on him, he stops for a moment to admire the marble sculpture of a young boy on the pedestal to his right—art is simply everywhere in Florence. He could get lost here—or, he wonders, is he already lost here?

In the heavy summer heat he walks across the Ponte Vecchio, past the leather and jewelry merchants, wending his way toward the hotel where Brea waits for him. The events of the summer strike him and weaken him like a sudden flu.

He'd known about Brea's infidelity the moment he saw her on stage with Sam. Why has he been unable to confront her? Is it because he needed to get through his talk first? Or is it that he's hoping it is not true? She has looked at him these past few days in a hesitant way, wanting to tell him, he knows, wanting to unburden herself, perhaps wanting to explain. But he hasn't given her any openings. He knows it's selfish on his part. Or is it his way of punishing her? Punishing himself? He believes she hasn't been disloyal to him before. Why now? Why?

When it becomes too painful to think about Brea and what he must soon say to her, he thinks of his father and what Eva Hathaway revealed about him in her journal. What is the truth? Will he ever know? Had Eva transferred onto his father her need for human warmth and affection in the wake of her parents' traumatic murder-suicide? If so, his father most likely never actually touched her. Had she been sexually abused when she was younger? Had it been his father's unorthodox style of conducting a therapy—willing Eva to imagine he was touching her? Or in truth had his father sexually abused Eva? Will he ever know? Perhaps Philip, as Eva's new psychiatrist, will ferret out what happened?

It is too intolerable to think that his father had been capable of abusing one of his patients. It is easier to believe it was his unconventional therapeutic approach. But even if that was the case, his father had been unethical in creating such a false therapeutic relationship.

His father was a hypocrite—his dedication to his patients had been a sham!

Stephen's head throbs—the more he reviles his father, the more it hurts. A thought suddenly darts through his mind—had Eva's aunt Lora been the grand passion of his father's life? His father had been obsessed with her. So the enigmatic patron who tipped so well at Happenings—Mr. Green—had been his father! Why had he stayed with his mother? Had he grown tired of Lora Casamassima? Perhaps he had not really loved her. Maybe he'd been incapable of loving anyone.

Stephen's memory of his father is now jumbled, painfully so. Arthur Forester hadn't been perfect; he'd been all too fallible, perhaps criminally so. But what saddens Stephen so deeply is that all along he'd been convinced his vision of his father was whole and complete. He'd been a sightless David to his father, his Goliath.

He looks out at the Arno—as murky as the Mississippi, he thinks. In frustration, he takes his phone from his pocket. Has Brea tried to call him? Nothing. Instead, there is an e-mail from Philip.

Stephen,

Just finished my second session with E.H. Did you know Happenings was closed down a year after the parents' murder-suicide when police discovered it was a front for a child abuse ring? In fact, your father was called to testify at the investigation. E.H. seems not to know anything about this. We can have no further communication about her case because she's expressly forbidden me to do so. P.B.

He puts back his phone, and stops walking. As he looks out again at the Arno, trying to digest Philip's words, it dawns on him that Eva must have been sexually abused as a child at Happenings. Then there was his father, his actions! He can no longer rationalize, no longer deny what he knows is true. It was not transference—it had been real; his father had fondled Eva.

He's no longer living partially in the dark, yet the light is harsh and antiseptic, as if he has awakened in a dentist's chair.

But why? This other side of his father will always remain a mystery to him, he thinks grievously. He'll always lack complete knowledge. Certain questions will never be answered. Not knowing the entire story—isn't that part of the human condition?

Twenty-Five

Brea and Stephen, late August

In the late summer heat of Florence, Brea and Stephen, having just finished lunch at an outdoor restaurant in the Piazza della Signoria, linger over espressos.

Woozy from the wine they drank with their meal and the warmth of the afternoon sun, they are hesitant at one moment, free flowing the next. To someone observing them, they would appear to be a somewhat contented couple, possibly American, perhaps a little more subdued than most; they keep their voices low, as if not to draw attention to themselves. She wears large oval-shaped dark glasses, and he has clipped on shades over his eyeglasses.

This onlooker may wonder if there is any passion between them. Does he or she have any sense of the emotional storm that transpired between the couple a few days earlier? Is it apparent there has been any strife?

After his talk at the conference, Stephen went to their hotel room and confronted Brea. At first she was relieved it was out in the open, deeply regretting she hadn't been able to speak first. She stood in the middle of the room, a tissue in one of her clenched hands, anguished, her body fatigued as she explained in detail what happened between her and Sam. She assured Stephen it had only happened once, and it happened because she'd been too open, and yes, edgy.

When she finished speaking, she sat down on the side of the bed and told Stephen, her deep brown eyes meeting his green gaze, her voice fervent, that she did love him—but she looked more rattled than anything else. She lowered her head, pressing one hand to her forehead.

Stephen's eyes clouded. He went over to her, sat next to Brea, wrapping his arms around her. He was the one to blame, he said, his voice sober. Maybe he'd been pushing her to Sam all along. He'd driven her away this summer by becoming too preoccupied with his work. Though he'd believed he'd been listening to her all along, he had stubbornly refused to understand her anguish. Yes, she had been and would continue to be much stronger than he was or would ever be. He rested his chin on her shoulder. Then he told her, his voice soft and pensive, what he had learned about his father. As he spoke, she grew still. When he finished, she turned toward him and held him close, not saying a word.

They did not leave their hotel room for the entire day, distractedly welcoming the waiters bringing food, leaving trays with half-eaten salads, untouched bowls of soup, and empty wine glasses outside their door. There were moments when they clung together in tears, and at other times they didn't speak at all, just stared straight ahead as if they were lost in a darkening forest, looking for a ray of light to guide them out. In the early morning hours they made love, feeling hesitant at first, bonding at last.

Can the onlooker notice an aura of calm hovering over this couple now? Calm after the storm?

Stephen, before taking another sip of espresso, says, "Brea, if you're unhappy in Harrington, I won't deter you, though it may take longer than a year for us to move. A practice is difficult to close, but I know so many people in New York—it won't be difficult for me to go back."

Brea smiles bemusedly. "I've come to another conclusion—we'll be okay no matter where we are. I've realized I wanted to return to New York to relive my youth. And isn't happiness an illusion, Stephen? Haven't I been naïve? I am content. Is there more? But if you feel the need to go back to New York, in two years Ned will be starting high school, and it wouldn't be a bad time to move. I can't say I'd be opposed to the idea."

"I guess we'll have to see," Stephen says lightly, but feels a lump in his throat as he thinks of Mrs. Alving's words, the line Brea had ardently practiced: *I thought you understood where I'd lost what you call my heart at the time.*

Her relationship with Sam will never be spoken about again; it is between them. It is something which they will cope with and eventually transcend because they do want their life together to move on. It will cause them a sense of anxiety for a while but it will dissipate as they both look forward to their future.

After finishing their espressos, they cross the street and hail a cab. They plan to do some more sightseeing and it is too hot to walk.

"Galleria dell'Accademia," Stephen says to the flushed taxi driver.

There is a hush inside the Accademia, reminding Stephen of his study in the early morning hours. He feels a sudden ache to be home, to see Ned.

They are both entranced by the marble statues surrounding them. Tears spring to Brea's eyes as she takes in the beauty of the works. When she gazes up at the *David*, she gasps. She is struck by the expression in his eyes, the strength, the longing—determination overcoming fear. Then she remembers. She turns to look for Stephen and finds him studying a statue of an old bearded man.

"Stephen let me take your photo—isn't there one of you as a boy standing in front of the *David*? Yes, the picture of you on the desk in your study." She takes Stephen by the hand.

Now before the *David*, she quickly looks about to make certain there is no guard watching her, and pulls out a camera from her straw bag.

Stephen puts his hand over the lens; in a soft voice, he says, "Brea, no—not again."

Twenty-Six

Stephen, early September

Dear Dr. Forester,

As you have suggested, I've gone to Dr. Barone, and have seen him four or five times over the past few weeks. I realize I have much work to do, much more than I fathomed when I last spoke with you. Because I had known your father, my therapy with you was never able to progress; you could never truly be my psychiatrist.

Dr. Barone remembers having read years ago about my parent's murder-suicide. He was in his third year of medical school at the time, and your father had discussed the case with him and the other students. At first, I was doubtful. I didn't know whether I should see Dr. Barone any longer. But as he had been forthright with the information, and because I had intuitively trusted Dr. Barone when I first met him, the fact that he had been a student of your father's and had known about the case has not prevented me from continuing to see him. He also promised he would not consult with you about my case. And that is what I found most reassuring.

Still I write in my journal; rarely do I miss a day. By now you must have read the pages I left on your desk. You needed to know the truth, I thought, and still do. Though with help from Dr. Barone, I realize more and more that there are many layers to what I call the truth. And so the truth is more difficult to know, more difficult than I imagined. Yet through writing in my journal and my sessions with Dr. Barone, and though it may take years, I believe I will be whole. Dr. Barone has also explained to me how one's brain can be injured after a traumatic emotional event, like one's arm or leg following a physical assault. And in the case of the brain, one's perceptions and memories can be thrown, so to speak, out of joint. Yet as of now, this day, I believe your father was an evil man. Because of what he'd done to me, I felt an overwhelming sense of guilt. I am neither dark nor evil. I hope I do not sound too harsh, but I am feeling a bit rough around the edges.

Regards,
E.H.

Stephen puts the letter in the top drawer of his desk, and glances at the photo of himself in front of Michelangelo's *David*. Then he goes over to the window and watches Ned out on the front lawn, playing wiffle ball with a friend.

When Eva had spoken about the small room in the back of the nightclub, he should have realized what had happened to her there, he thinks. She was sexually abused as a child at Happenings, and has blocked it completely from her mind.

Because she'd been abused in the past she accepted his father's behavior during their sessions, never uttered a word about it until she revealed it to her first husband. She had told Stephen early on about her bruise. Yet she'd been bruised again and again all her life, he thinks. Through her work with Philip, he's confident she'll realize what she experienced at Happenings. It may take years, but she will eventually know. And that is what she'd been looking for when she first came to him—the truth.

When he returned from Italy, he had checked and discovered that although his father had had to testify, he had not been involved in the sex abuse scandal at Happenings; neither were her parents. They must have been in denial about it all; her mother, he guesses, more fleetingly aware than her father, who simply drank. But they couldn't leave Happenings—the atmosphere there was like a drug. So her father drank more and more, and her mother became more and more anxious. Maybe one day they inadvertently discovered what was going on at Happenings and realized their daughter may have been affected. And it just wore them down.

What his father had done to Eva was criminal. How many other patients had he abused? He shudders. And he had so harshly judged his mother, had secretly blamed her for years for his anxious nature. But his insecurities had existed because of his father's behavior, not his mother's. Hopefully she had found comfort for a while in the arms of someone who had been a member of her political group. But not Philip— Philip had been her friend. It is all so clear now, he thinks.

His one personal regret in all this is his mother. If only he'd known, he could have stood by her, encouraged her to leave his father. Always, it is better to know, he thinks, and checks his watch. Brea will be coming home soon from an audition in Boston. He wants to hear how it went. He doesn't want to make the same mistake twice, he thinks. He goes back to his desk, takes another look at the photo of himself in front of the *David,* and switches off the light.

Twenty-Seven

Eva, mid-September

She is pleased she's written to Dr. Forester, and imagines him reading her letter, holding it close to his hazy green eyes, longing to discover the truth in her words. But she has since realized that not only are there many layers to the truth, there are many truths, and focusing on one alone while ignoring the others will lead you astray.

Briskly she walks up the front stone steps of the office building where she'll meet with Dr. Barone. As she crosses the high-ceilinged lobby she notices an out-of-order sign on the elevator door. On an aluminum stand nearby there is another sign with an arrow pointing in the opposite direction. She walks in a semicircle to the other side of the building, near the old, boarded-up entranceway. Beyond a wide doorway she finds the stairway.

After taking the first three steps, she experiences a compelling sense of familiarity. Suddenly dizzy, she reaches for the banister. It is the same building where she'd met with Dr. Arthur Forester. She'd come in through the old entranceway, opening the heavy oak door.

Closing her eyes, she sees herself as she was—seventeen-year-old Eva Morelli wearing an unbuttoned navy-blue trench coat, the strap of her shoulder bag across her chest, her long dark hair flowing down her back. She'd walk up the stairway in fear, her blue-gray eyes misty, her lips parched, not knowing what to expect from the great doctor, as her aunt called him.

Now she wants to turn around and leave, but she can't—she's trapped! She presses her hand to her heart, stands there frozen for what she believes is the longest time. When she is steady, she looks down, stares hard at the banister; it is old and chipped, not shiny and polished as it was all those years ago. Arthur Forester is dead, she reminds herself. This is another century. She's not going to his office, but will see Philip Barone—on a different floor—someone who has not harmed her, someone who has simply listened to her. But most importantly, she's helped herself—slowly the old Eva and the new are becoming one. Her sorrow recedes; her strength returns. She climbs upward.

CPSIA information can be obtained
at www.ICGtesting.com
Printed in the USA
EDOW031134240513
1688ED